Macklin

C.M. CURTIS

kwympublishing.com
info@kwympublishing.com

1st Edition
Cover Design by KWYM Publishing, LLC

ISBN-13: 978-1539194446
ISBN-10: 1539194442

Contents

C.M. CURTIS

CHAPTER 1

"Looks to me like somebody mistook this jasper's head for a piece of firewood and took an axe to it."

"Been shot, too. Don't know as I ever seen a man who was kilt like this."

"He ain't dead."

"He's as dead as Columbus. Flies is already gatherin' around him."

"They're gatherin' around you too, and you're alive."

"He's dead, all right. Listen close and you can hear angels a singin' him home."

"Bet me."

"Bet you what? You ain't got nothin' I want."

"Well, if you're afraid to bet . . ."

"Ain't that I'm afraid, I just know what you're after, Howie."

"Don't see why it would hurt a man to offer a swig of his whiskey to an old friend, but if you ain't sure of yourself, then don't bet."

"Oh, I'm sure, all right. This ranny's dead."

"So it's a bet?"

"One swig."

"One swig's fine. I ain't a greedy man, Bill."

Bill gave a snort of derision and said, "Now you got the burden of proof, 'cause if I ever seen a dead man, this is one."

Howie grinned in greedy triumph, "See right here? Right there on his neck, now watch."

"I don't see nothin'."

"That's cause you're not tryin'. You just watch."

With the tops of their heads almost touching, the two kneeling men bent low to look at the subject's neck. Suddenly Howie cried in triumph, "See there? See there?"

Bill straightened, "I didn't see nothin'." But the look on his face and the lack of conviction in his voice said otherwise, and they were enough for Howie, who held out a gloating hand.

"One swig," said Bill sharply.

If Howie's idea of a swig had ever gained general acceptance, subsequent generations of school children would have been taught there were ten swigs to a gallon. Bill was scowling when he received the bottle back, but he made no comment.

"Now, what do we do with him?" said Howie, wiping his mouth in satisfaction.

Bill's mood was now somewhat less than benevolent. He said, "Why do anything? He ain't our problem."

"He'll be our problem if somebody follers our tracks here and tries to blame us for killin' him."

"Then we'll have to wait 'til he dies and bury him," said Howie.

Bill looked around at the rocky terrain and, seeing nothing that looked like easy digging, decided on an easier course. He said, "All right, we'll drop him off at the undertaker. He'll be dead by the time we get him there."

"How we going to get him to town?"

"You ride over to Milo Barnes' place and borrow his wagon."

"Why don't you ride over to Milo Barnes' place?"

"'Cause I want you to."

"But I want you to."

There was a long pause as they both considered the stalemate. Then Bill said, "Halfers?"

Howie grinned and reached in the man's vest and pulled out a gold watch, and the two men started going through the man's pockets.

~⚬⚬~

Marshal Johnny Belmont was never happy to see Bill and Howie, but he was even less so today when they showed him what they had in the back of the borrowed wagon.

"Take him over to the undertaker," he said.

"Undertaker or doctor? You tell us," said Howie, "'cause five miles back he was still alive."

"Looks dead to me."

"That's what I thought too," said Bill, still bitter about his whiskey. "Turned out he was alive."

Marshal Belmont looked at the man in the wagon, shook his head and gave a low whistle. "Where'd he fall from, the moon?"

"He didn't fall from anywhere. He was lyin' out on a flat spot away from anything higher than a prickly pear."

Now, the marshal's face showed interest. "You mean somebody did this to him?"

"Well there weren't no bear tracks around."

The marshal looked closer at the man and said, "Looks pretty dead. Take him over to Doc Pope's. Let him decide."

Bill started to whip the reins, but the marshal raised his hand. "Find anything in his pockets? I imagine you checked 'em."

"Why sure, we checked 'em like a man naturally would when he was tryin' to help, but there was nothin' there. Whoever done this to him must have cleaned him out before we come along."

Skepticism showed on the marshal's face, but he said, "Get him over to Doc Pope's. Tell him I'll talk to him later."

The doctor had gone out to visit a patient, and his wife had gone with him as she often did. Clara Teel, the doctor's assistant, however, was in. She checked the man in the back of the wagon, and declared him to be alive—though she did not understand how—and instructed Bill and Howie to carry him inside.

Clara was an attractive widow in her late thirties, competent and thorough, stern but compassionate. She had followed her husband to Tombstone where he had opened a business. During its heyday, Tombstone suffered several devastating fires, and Sid Teel's business fell victim to the first one. Nearly bankrupt, he invested the remainder of his money in a mining venture that failed. Feeling he had been swindled, he argued with one of his partners and the argument turned into a gunfight in which Teel was killed.

Forced to find a way to support herself, Clara, who had some nursing experience, was able to get a job as Doctor Pope's assistant. And, after seeing her work, the doctor felt lucky to have her.

It was a rough town they lived in in this rough corner of Arizona, and Clara had seen men who had been injured in almost every imaginable way. She had seen plenty of men who had been beaten, but never one who had been beaten this badly. It seemed impossible that he could still be alive and more unlikely still that he would live to see tomorrow. But life or death decisions were not up to Clara and she set about doing her work in the most thorough way she could.

She heard the front door open and boots on the floor of the front room. She called over her shoulder, "Sit down. I'll be with you in a minute."

"It's me, Clara." She recognized the voice of Marshal Johnny Belmont.

"I'm in here," she said.

He came in and stood for a moment, looking at the inert figure of the man lying on the bed. Clara was sponging his wounds, which were many. Scarcely a part of his body had escaped some form of damage.

"Any idea who he is?" she asked.

"How would you tell?" said Belmont. "Could be anybody . . . my brother or your dead husband come back to life and nobody'd recognize him." He shook his head, "I never saw anything like this."

"Me neither."

"Think he'll make it?"

Clara was too professional to answer such a question in the presence of a patient, even if the patient was unconscious, but she looked at the marshal and gave a slight shake of the head.

The night passed and morning came and still the patient clung to life. Doctor Pope, on his return the previous night, had examined the man and agreed there was no reason he shouldn't be dead and no reason to suspect he may pull through. A man simply couldn't survive such injuries.

∼ ∾ ∾∽

No man wants to die, but Dave Macklin understood better than most people that there were worse things, and as he watched the distant Apaches who were, he knew, trying to pick up his trail, he tried to decide what to do if they got too close and capture became inevitable.

Why couldn't they just kill a man and be done with it? he asked himself. Was it because the brutality of their environment had somehow infused itself into their tissues and made them as brutal as their harsh, desert surroundings? He pondered this for a moment, then made his decision and put it out of his mind.

He glanced at the sun, so agonizingly slow in its transit from horizon to horizon. There were still hours to be endured before sundown brought darkness and some relief from the merciless heat. Anything could happen in those hours. If he could remain undetected until darkness came, Macklin believed he had a good chance of escaping. If his horse weren't already half dead from exhaustion and thirst, he would have an even better chance.

Well, he reflected, a man made a gamble when he traveled alone in Apache country. He had taken his chances and now he would accept without complaint whatever came. But he would fight for all he was worth until the very end, until that very last bullet—the one he was saving for himself.

Macklin's eyes burned from the heat, from the dryness of the air, from the brightness of the sun, and from constantly scanning the desert, watching every tiny wisp of dust that arose from the land either from natural or human activity.

Dust. The natural telegraph of the desert. It could be seen, smelled, even tasted. It told of the presence of friend or enemy, advising direction and speed of travel, even size of group. And even Apaches, clever as they were, could not, when mounted, avoid stirring some of it up.

Macklin felt himself growing drowsy. He imagined how good it would feel just to close his eyes and rest for a while. Normally it would be hard for a man to sleep in this kind of heat, but Dave Macklin was profoundly weary and he had to fight to stay awake.

A corner of his vision caught a rise of dust that could only be coming from the hoofs of a running animal. Soon that animal came into his field of view and he immediately recognized old Deacon George, riding on that broken-down mare of his. And the deacon was being pursued by a mounted Apache.

Macklin could clearly see that George was not going to make it. He was whipping his horse furiously with the reins, kicking it frantically and swearing at it in a hoarse, panicked way. What was the old fool doing out in the desert alone anyway? Macklin wondered, and then he answered his own question. There were hundreds of men out in this desert prospecting for gold and silver, each of them hoping to be the next Ed Schieffelin.

The sun flashed off the knife the Apache held in his hand as he gained on the old, grunting mare. In his mind, Macklin could see the end clearly. The Apache would come up alongside Deacon George and use the knife; probably not in a lethal way, and George would be taken alive.

And the Apaches would eat the mare tonight.

Swearing under his breath at Deacon George, Macklin slid his carbine into position, clicked the hammer back, and, resting it on a flat rock in front of him, took aim. He would not try to hit the Apache—that would be too chancy at this range. The horse was a much bigger target.

Because of the distance, he would have to aim high, to compensate for the drop of the bullet, and slightly ahead of the horse, to let him run into it.

He took his aim, moving the barrel horizontally, just enough to keep up with the running horse. He squeezed the trigger and the rifle kicked against his shoulder. A fraction of a second later, the Apache was thrown from the horse by the unseen bullet.

Despite the circumstances, Macklin laughed out loud. "Missed the pony and hit the Indian," he said to himself as he ran for his horse. He had left the poor brute saddled, against the need of a quick getaway, and now all he had to do was quickly tighten the cinch and leap into the saddle. He had betrayed his position by firing the shot, and now his life depended on this jaded, undernourished, dehydrated animal.

The Apaches knew every water hole, seep, or spring in this desert, and every spot of grass where a horse could be picketed to graze. Their ponies were fresh, well-fed, and well-watered. How, Macklin asked himself, could his horse be expected to outrun them?

Topping a small rise, he looked back and was not surprised to see the Apaches coming after him. He brutally spurred his horse and whipped it with the reins, trying not to think about what he was asking the animal to do. The Apaches would have no pity on him if they captured him, and he must have no pity on this horse.

Every time Macklin looked back, he saw the Apaches had gained on him. He wondered how Deacon George's old mare was doing. She had looked pretty near the point of collapse when he had shot the apache. But the deacon was ahead of him somewhere, Macklin knew. He could taste the man's dust.

His horse's breathing was becoming more labored; its pace was faltering. It wouldn't be long now. He began looking for a place to make a stand, but not with much optimism. The best he could hope for would be to hold them off until nightfall when they would creep up and surround him.

The trail he was on began angling downward into a broad, shallow valley, perhaps eight miles wide. Now he saw a good deal of dust ahead of him. Judging by its amount and pattern, it could only be one of two things: a train of freight wagons or a detail of mounted cavalry.

As he approached he saw that it was the former. Freighters had begun traveling in groups because the Apaches were out. Each wagon carried at least two teamsters, and they were well-armed.

Ahead of him, he saw Deacon George come up to the wagons and as the wagons drew up and their dust began to dissipate, he saw the deacon waving and gesticulating, pointing in his direction.

The freight wagons immediately began forming up in a circle. Macklin felt a small glimmer of hope. He looked back and judged the distance and speed of the pursuing Apaches and realized that if his laboring horse could last a little longer, he might just reach the wagons before the Indians caught him.

The Apaches apparently had more faith in his mount than he did, because when he looked back, he saw that they had stopped and were watching him pull away from them. One young Apache, however—probably anxious to prove himself—continued forward, kicking his horse in the flanks and shouting guttural Apache words. His fresh horse was coming up fast. Macklin understood the young man's intent—he would try to make a quick kill, take a scalp, and flee before the teamsters could do anything.

Macklin reined in, swung out of the saddle, and raised his Winchester, but before he could fire, some of the teamsters opened up. Several bullets hit their mark just as the Apache's pony leaped over a narrow wash bed. The animal landed on the other side on limp legs, smashed to the ground, and rolled. The young Apache rolled free and stumbled to his feet, but another volley of shots put him to the ground a few feet away from his pony.

Macklin stood by his horse and watched as the Apaches turned and rode away. They would return later for the body of their friend, he knew.

Leading his lathered horse, he walked across to the circle of wagons, where some of the teamsters were taking advantage of the stop to water their mules. Macklin's horse staggered as it walked, its sides heaving in and out. He stripped off the saddle and, having received permission from one of the teamsters, threw it on top of a tarp-covered wagon.

"Close scrape," commented the teamster.

Macklin nodded. Motioning to one of the water barrels that was ironed to the side of the wagon, he said, "Could you spare some water for my horse?"

Once the horse had quit blowing, Macklin allowed it to drink, rationing the water so the animal didn't drink too much too fast. Afterward he gratefully accepted a canteen offered to him by one of the teamsters and drank his fill.

Deacon George came over, leading his old mare, which was not in much better shape than Macklin's horse. He said proudly, "Folks say she's old, but she outrun them Apaches right smart. I thought one of 'em was goin' to catch up to us, but then I looked back and he wasn't there. Right smart she outrun 'em." He patted the old mare lovingly and said, "You come pretty close to shoutin' hallelujah out there yourself, didn't you Dave?"

"Closer than I like," replied Macklin.

They both rode on one of the freight wagons, perched on top of the cargo, their horses tied to the back. Both animals were too exhausted to be ridden. Macklin's horse was ruined, he knew, and the thought saddened him.

Few words were spoken on the ride to town, but just before they got there, Deacon George shook his head and said, "That good old mare of mine. She sure outrun them Apache's ponies, she did. Wisht you'd been there to see it, Dave."

"Yep," said Macklin.

⁓

Clara Teel was both surprised and pleased when her patient was still alive after the second night. But when Doctor Pope checked him that morning, he shook his head and said, "Too much fever. That bullet wound is infected."

Clara sat up with the patient that night, frequently sponging his fevered brow and giving him sips of water.

Although he was not conscious, there was a sense of uneasiness about him. A sense that on some level he was suffering. At one point, late into the night, knowing nothing else to do for him, she took his hand and held it, lightly stroking it. Somehow this seemed to calm him and he rested easier.

Night after night she sat with him. Day after day she ministered to him, until one day the doctor sent her home and said, "I want you to sleep all night. I don't want to see you again until tomorrow. You're making yourself sick."

Clara only followed the doctor's orders partially. After five hours of sleep and an hour to bathe and freshen her appearance, she was back in the early morning. Her patient was still alive, but his color was worse than it had been. She sat in the chair by his bed and took his hand and began to sing softly, careful to keep her voice low enough not to wake the doctor or his wife.

At five thirty that morning, the doctor came in wearing his bed clothes and checked the patient. "I think he may be a little better. Whatever you're doing, Clara, keep doing it."

And Clara did keep doing it. Day after day, night after night, with brief breaks for rest and meals. She and the doctor became convinced that when she was with the patient, holding his hand and talking or singing softly to him, his condition improved. When she was away from his side, it worsened.

When the freight wagons pulled into town, Macklin said a quick adios to Deacon George, jumped down, and, thanking the teamster, untied his horse from the back of the wagon. At the livery stable he told Harvey Downs, the liveryman, to do what he could for the poor animal.

Harvey was a man who had worked with horses all his life. It only took one glance for him to know the story. "Apaches?" he said.

"Good guess," said Dave Macklin.

"You'll be needing another one."

"What have you got?"

Downs told him and Macklin said, "Too much. I can't afford it. How much will you give me for this one?"

Downs snorted, "How much would you give for him?"

"Not a cent."

"Funny thing. That's the exact figure I had in mind," said Downs. Then he added, "I thought you had a whole herd of horses you were going to sell to the army."

"Apaches got 'em all. Every last one of 'em."

"And tried to take your hair too, eh."

"And came pretty close to gettin' it."

Downs was pensive for a moment, then he said, "I'll give you three dollars for him and I'll be takin' a risk at that. If he don't perk up in a few days, he'll have to be shot and I'll be wantin' my three dollars back."

Glumly contemplating this reversal in his fortunes, Macklin walked down the main street of Contention City. He was a broad-shouldered man, a little over six-feet tall in his boots and a little under without them. His light-brown hair was longer at the moment than he was accustomed to wearing it and he mentally debated whether or not to get a haircut before the party tonight. He had a three-day's growth of whiskers on his face that he would shave off when he got his bath.

Like all the towns in the Tombstone area—like Tombstone itself—Contention City was a brand-new town. Two years earlier this spot had been dirt and rocks and brush. But water had not yet been discovered at Tombstone and reduction mills needed water to operate, so the ore-milling towns of Charleston and Contention City had been built along the San Pedro River to serve the mines in the area.

The river provided the only real greenery in the town—a long stripe of verdure in a brown desert. The trees and grass and bushes that grew on its banks were, like the water itself, soothing to the eyes of any traveler who arrived here, having crossed the desert with its drab and washed-out colors. The buildings here were mostly of adobe or stone or a combination thereof, and though they were new, they were just as dull as their surroundings.

To those who came from wetter climates, the San Pedro was nothing impressive. One new arrival had said to Macklin, "Where I come from, that would be called a creek, not a river."

During most of the year, it was a shallow, slow-moving body of water, easily waded by human or horse alike, and even during the wetter times of year, it was nothing formidable, but in this desert it was an entity of huge importance.

In Contention City there were, of course, several saloons, as well as a general merchandise store, a restaurant and various other businesses to serve the inhabitants of the town.

Many of the millworkers, like the men who worked in nearby mines, lived in tents around the town, while others slept in the flophouses that had sprung up, along with the other businesses that catered to the working men. Some of the men, mainly those few who had brought their families, had built their own houses, paying local Mexican laborers to make the adobe bricks and sometimes to lay them up as well.

Contention's main street was not a long one and Dave Macklin did not have to walk far to reach the town marshal's office. He immediately stepped inside.

Marshal Johnny Belmont was sitting at his desk, a magazine on his chest, his head leaned back, dozing in his chair. A plate with a half-finished meal sat on his desk next to his dusty, worn boots. He woke, saw Macklin, and scowled. He looked Macklin up and down and said, "You look like a tramp. If you can't come to town looking any better than that, you ought not come at all."

Macklin said, "I'd like to see you unpin that star and come around here and say that to me."

The marshal drew his tall, lanky frame to a standing position, took off the badge, and came around, assuming a boxer's stance, and the two men began sparring and laughing, acting like two young boys.

Finally the marshal stepped back and said, "All right, what is it? You already owe me thirty-five dollars. What do you need this time?"

Macklin went around the desk, sat in the chair, and began eating the food Belmont had left on the plate. Around a mouthful he said, "I need to borrow a suit and a boiled shirt for the party tonight."

"What's wrong with yours?"

"Some Apache brave is probably wearing 'em right now to impress his squaw."

The marshal grew sober. "They hit your place?"

"Burned it."

"Get your horses?"

"Every last one except the one I was riding, and he's not worth shooting now."

"Close one, was it?"

Macklin shrugged. "I'll go to bed with my hair on tonight. Could've been worse."

"Not that keepin' your hair does you much good," said the marshal. "You're still the ugliest man in town."

"Second ugliest," argued Macklin, not looking up from the plate, "right behind you."

"Keep talkin' like that and you'll go to Sally's party wearing what you're wearing right now. By the way, you got any money on you?"

"Not much. I've got a pretty good stash buried in a can under the floor of my house, but . . ." He left the rest unsaid. Macklin's stash was a considerable sum of money and Belmont was probably the only person he knew to whom he would confide its existence, much less its location. Johnny Belmont was that kind of friend.

Belmont nodded. "No good gettin' scalped tryin' to get your money." He fished in his pocket and pulled out a double eagle.

"Thanks," said Macklin. "I'll pay you back as soon as I can."

"Yes, you will," said Belmont, "or I'll arrest you." Then he added, "Might as well stay at my place, since you're too broke to afford a hotel room."

"I was already figurin' on that. I take my breakfast in bed, around nine o'clock."

Belmont snorted, "We only do that for prisoners." He paused and said, "If you get too far down on your luck, I'll arrest you to save you from starvin' to death."

"I'd rather starve to death than listen to that racket all day and all night."

"What racket?"

"You don't even hear it anymore, do you?"

"You mean the stamp mill? You get so you don't notice it. In fact, when it shuts down for repairs, it seems too quiet."

"I like the quiet better. Out at my place it's so quiet you can hear the flappin' of a butterfly's wings."

"Apaches can be pretty quiet, too," Belmont reminded him.

Macklin went to one of the bathhouses the miners and millworkers used. He didn't mind using their bathhouse, as long as he could pay extra for clean, unused water, but he refused to sleep in their lice-infested flophouses.

Clean and freshly shaved and wearing clean long johns he had purchased before going to the bathhouse, he went to the small adobe structure Belmont called home and slept for three hours. Later, wearing Marshal Johnny Belmont's spare suit, which was a little long in the legs and a little tight in the shoulders, he stopped in at one of the several saloons in town. His three hours of sleep had reinvigorated him mentally and physically, a testament to his iron constitution and youthful vitality, but his ordeal in the desert had left him with an insatiable need for fluid and he stepped up to the bar and ordered a beer.

The beer was warm, of course—there was no ice in Contention, except maybe at Sally Pennington's party tonight—but he savored each mouthful as though it were a new experience. The story of his narrow escape from the Apaches had spread around town, and several men came over and sat with him, asking him questions. All of them agreed he had been exceedingly fortunate.

They were not jocular today, as men normally tend to be in saloons; the knowledge that they too were susceptible to attack by Indians was having a distinctly sobering effect on them, and for a time they sat discussing what they believed could be done, needed to be done, hadn't been done in the past, and was not being done now. It was generally agreed that the army should send soldiers west in greater numbers to end this Apache problem once and for all.

Macklin listened, not saying much. He had little interest in the way things ought to be but weren't. As the other men talked and disputed, his mind ran forward to the party tonight. There was a particular young lady he was anxious to see, though he knew full well he was being a fool; the young lady could not possibly have any interest in him. And why should she? What did he have to offer her? Whatever prospects he had had for the future had just been stolen by Apaches.

Finished with his beer, he excused himself and started to leave the saloon, intending to go to Hopkins' Restaurant for a meal. But after consulting his pocket watch, it occurred to him that there would be a good amount of food at Sally Pennington's party tonight, and it would be far better food than any he would find in any of the restaurants in town. So he snatched half a sandwich from the saloon's free lunch counter to remove the sharpest edge of his hunger until it could be fully sated at the party.

He had a little time to kill, and he walked over to the livery stable to check on his horse. The news was not good. "We'll know in a couple of days," said the stableman.

Macklin spent about a half hour lavishing attention on the poor brute, brushing it and rubbing it down. Nothing he did would make any major difference in the long run, but the animal had saved his life and what little he could do for it he would do.

Leaving the stable, he noticed two young children, a boy and a girl sitting dejectedly on the edge of the boardwalk next to a watering trough. The two were known to Macklin, and he walked over and sat down beside them and, without any difficulty at all, extracted from them their tale of woe.

Mandy, the older of the two Carlson children, related that she and her brother, Todd, had been asked by one of the town's leading citizens, Herman Chilter, proprietor of the butcher shop, to round up several stray head of his cattle that had escaped through a broken fence. And for that service, he had promised to pay them six bits. They had done so but had made the mistake of approaching him for payment in the presence of his wife, Elona, who had immediately put a halt to the transaction, giving the children some penny candy instead and then shooing them on their way.

The children lived with their grandfather and their older sister, and they had promised they would be bringing the six bits home and now were reluctant to go home empty-handed.

Frowning, Macklin looked down the street in the direction of the butcher shop. It was like Elona Chilter to do such a thing, and it was like Herman, who was a decent man but was unable to stand up to his domineering wife, to permit it to happen.

He fished in his pocket, regretting the money he had spent on beer, and withdrew some change. He counted out six bits and handed it to the children. "Don't tell your grandpa about this," he said.

The two youngsters thanked him and left on the run.

Dave Macklin had never understood why Sally Pennington invited him to her parties. But she did and he wasn't complaining about it. The food was always delicious to the palate, and the colorful furnishings in Sally's large and expensive home were delicious to eyes accustomed to the muted tones of the desert vegetation and landscape.

Mrs. Pennington was a wealthy widow whose husband had owned a mine and a reduction mill. After his death, Mrs. Pennington had sold the mine, but she still owned the mill, and its rumbling sound could be heard in town twenty-four hours a day.

Marshal Johnny Belmont was already at the party and he hailed Macklin from across the spacious front room of the house. But before Macklin could cross, Sally Pennington came in from another room. She was a short woman, and her heavy figure attested to her love of food. She had sold her husband's mine for a sum that she realized she would never be able to spend in her lifetime and had turned the mill over to her three sons to run, while she turned her attention to directing the construction of the huge house in which she now resided and in which she held her frequent parties.

Coming up to Macklin and shaking his hand, she said, "It's good to see you, Mr. Macklin, with all your bones intact and your scalp still in place."

Warmed by her reception, Macklin smiled broadly. "Oh, those Apaches didn't mean me any harm, Mrs. Pennington. They just wanted to ask me if I could finagle them an invitation to your party. Everybody in the territory wants to be here."

This delighted Sally Pennington, and she laughed as loudly as a woman of her grace and breeding could permit herself in such a setting. One of her servants had come out of the kitchen and now touched Sally on the shoulder. Sally turned, and the servant said something. Sally patted her on the arm and said, "It's all right. I'll be there in a minute." Turning back to Macklin, she said, "Enjoy yourself, Mr. Macklin. I'm glad you're here."

Macklin crossed to where Johnny Belmont was standing with several other men, listening to Deacon George tell the story of his escape from the Apaches.

"One of them red devils was right behind me, and they shot at me too. I thought I was a gone goose, but she outran him. My good old mare outran him." He turned to Macklin. "Didn't she, Dave?"

"Seemed like it," said Macklin neutrally.

No one seemed to notice the noncommittal manner in which Macklin made the statement, except Johnny Belmont, who knew him better than any other person alive. He gazed at Macklin speculatively for a moment. The deacon had finished his story and now had begun repeating parts of it.

Macklin, having no interest in hearing the story repeated, turned away, looking for someone else to talk to. There were several people whom he knew, but they were all engaged in conversation and out of politeness he refrained from intruding. He scanned the room, searching for one person in particular who did not appear to be present, then he caught sight of her in a corner with a group of people, partially hidden from his view by one of them. He could not be sure, but it seemed as though she had just been looking at him and had quickly averted her gaze when she saw his eyes turn toward her. Did it mean anything? he wondered, or was he imagining things?

Johnny Belmont was at his side now, a glass of punch in his hand. He said, "What's the real story about Deacon George?"

"I'll tell you later, but if that mare was twice as fast as she is, she still wouldn't have outrun that Apache."

Belmont chuckled and moved away.

Sally Pennington's house was designed for entertaining, for that was the thing Sally loved most. One spacious room flowed into another, which led to two other rooms, which flowed onto a veranda, which led into a maze-like garden with lamps hung all around and many secret places where there were benches for solitary contemplation and private conversations.

Macklin moved into the next room, where, on an elegant table, surrounded by a variety of different pastries on small plates, sat a huge punch bowl with chunks of ice floating in it. The ice, Macklin knew, had been freighted from the distant Huachuca Mountains, packed in burlap and straw.

The servant standing next to the table ladled a glass of punch for Macklin, and, sipping it, he casually moved through the room onto the veranda where he spoke briefly with someone he knew.

The call came for everyone to take their places at the two rows of long tables in Sally's enormous dining room, and Macklin followed the moving crowd, found his place, and sat down, finding himself seated between Deacon George and a matronly woman whose perfume threatened to overwhelm his keen, desert sense of olfaction.

Idly wondering who would be seated in the still-empty seat directly across from him, he casually scanned the group, hoping to catch a glimpse of Nan White, Sally Pennington's niece. Not seeing her, he turned back just as she took the seat in front of him. He rose politely and sat down again.

She smiled at him and gave a nod. He smiled and nodded back and spoke her name. And then his brain struggled to find something else to say. Had he known she would be seated across from him, he would have prepared comments and topics of conversation. Now, under pressure, he could think of nothing to say that would be worth saying, so he kept silent.

As the food was being served, he wondered if Nan's black hair naturally shone the way it did or if she used something on it: some kind of oil, perhaps, or a tea. How did she keep her complexion so flawless in the dry desert climate and why was it that a woman with such dark hair had such blue eyes? Such were his thoughts as his eyes moved around the room in an attempt to seem casual.

Presently Nan said, "I think we're supposed to make some effort at conversation."

Macklin felt himself blushing. "I'm sorry, I didn't mean to . . ." he struggled to think of the appropriate thing to say and all he could come up with was, "Yes, you're right."

She waited for a moment and he could have sworn there was a glint of humor in her eyes. She said, "So, tell us about your scrape with the Apaches."

The matronly woman on Macklin's right turned to him and said eagerly, "Yes, do tell us."

Before Macklin could utter a word, Deacon George, who had apparently been lost in thought, turned and, thinking the request had been directed at him, said, "Well, it was like this . . ." He flung himself wholeheartedly into a rendition of the story, which he had, though the events were less than a day old, already told enough times to have it memorized.

Thinking how the Apaches had unintentionally done Deacon George a very big favor, Macklin looked down at the table, and when he looked up again at Nan, she was looking straight at him. And the smile of delight and humor in her eyes was meant for him alone.

The food was every bit as wonderful as Macklin had expected it to be and dessert was just being served when there was a disturbance at the front door, one room away. Someone was shouting, demanding, ". . . Marshal . . . see him now . . . send him out, or we're comin' in."

Johnny Belmont, tall and lanky, was already on his feet, walking toward the door. Being the town marshal, he was wearing a gun. He was the only man in the room who was armed. Macklin rose and followed him.

Boots sounded on the floor in the next room, spurs jingled, and three men, looking out of place in their dusty, sweat-stained range clothes came into the dining room. They did not remove their hats. They smelled of sweat and horse and whiskey.

Marshal Belmont walked up to the one who was obviously their leader and said, "Doyle, let's take this outside. This is a party."

Frank Doyle was a big man, about fifty years old, with a long, untrimmed gray and red beard. He spoke, his voice loud and thick from anger and whiskey, "You've got two of my riders in your jail."

"Let's take it outside, Doyle," repeated Belmont.

"We'll take it right here," said Doyle in a harsh shout, "Here and now so everybody can hear what I've got to say. Double H is no two-bit, scrub outfit. We take care of our own people." He pointed a finger at Belmont. "One of my men causes trouble, you let me know. I'll horsewhip him or send him on his way. Double H does aplenty of business in this town, and we ought to get some respect for it. Texas men like to get a little rowdy now and then, which don't do no harm. A Double H man comes into town, has a little fun, don't hurt nobody, I expect you to leave him alone. You just send me word, and I'll take care of it." His voice softened somewhat in an attempt to be placatory, and he said, "Now, Marshal, I just want to hear you say that's the way it's goin' to be. You let my two boys out of jail, and we'll go on our way."

Belmont said, "Doyle, you're a long way from Texas. Maybe you were the big toad in the puddle there, but here the laws apply to everybody, no matter who they are or where they're from. You can run your ranch the way you want to, but don't come in here and tell us how to run our town."

Macklin had intentionally positioned himself at Belmont's left, standing so close their shoulders touched. Belmont knew why he was there, and he angled his body just a little in order to facilitate what Macklin was going to do.

Surreptitiously, with his right hand, Macklin reached into Belmont's left coat pocket and found the short-barreled .38 caliber pistol—the backup Belmont always carried—he knew would be there.

Using his body to shield the act, Macklin withdrew the pistol and, keeping his hand out of sight, held his arm pointed straight down, with the pistol hidden behind Belmont's leg.

Shouting obscenities, Doyle demanded, "I want those boys let out of jail now, Marshal."

"I won't do it," answered Belmont. "They broke the law."

Almost subconsciously, Macklin was aware of the fact that the people in the room had all moved to one side, and many of them had left the room to avoid catching a stray bullet.

There was a long, tense moment in which Macklin watched the three Texans. The small, wiry man on Doyle's right concerned him the most. He was twitchy. Now, his eyes quickly shuttled back and forth between Doyle and Belmont, and he growled, "Don't take that from him, Boss."

Macklin realized this man's nerves were set on a hair trigger. He was half drunk and was capable of taking matters into his own hands. Attentive to his every move and facial expression, Macklin also tried to keep one eye on Doyle, not knowing from where trouble would begin—if it began at all.

And then he saw Doyle relax. The Texan's hand moved a little distance from his gun, the tightness in his mouth loosened. Macklin thought the crisis was over. But at that moment, Elona Chilter came from the left, interposing herself between Macklin and the wiry Texan.

"You Texas trash, get out of here. Get out of here right now, all of you," she commanded.

It was like touching a match to a fuse. The wiry Texan went for his gun.

With the back of his left hand, Macklin struck Elona Chilter a wicked blow in the chest, knocking her out of the way. As he did so, his right hand swung up, cocking the .38. The wiry Texan's gun boomed, and out of the corner of his vision, Macklin was aware of

Johnny Belmont going down. Macklin's shot hit the Texan at the base of the throat.

Doyle's pistol was coming up, but Belmont's was already cocked, and as he was going down, he got off a shot that struck Doyle in the hip. The big Texan's aim was affected by this, and when he fired—a fraction of a second later—his shot missed Belmont and cut a groove in the floor. Macklin's second shot hit Doyle in the chest and the Texan dropped as though every nerve in his body had ceased functioning.

The Texan on Doyle's left had been slow in choosing a target. His pistol was out, but when the guns began booming, it unnerved him, and he fired a quick shot that went into the wall at the far end of the room. Now, re-cocking his pistol, he swung it toward Macklin, but Macklin already had the .38 lined up on him, and, seeing this, the Texan dropped his gun and threw up his hands, shouting, "I ain't in it! I ain't in it! Don't shoot!" He began backing away.

Seeing no threat now in this man, Macklin held his gun steady and watched as the man continued to back away and then turned and ran across the room and out the front door.

Macklin was not interested in following the fleeing man. He checked the two fallen Texans, both of whom were dead and then turned his attention to his friend on the floor. Suddenly he became aware of a good deal of noise in the room. Men were shouting, women were crying, there were shocked exclamations. Over to one side, Macklin could hear Elona Chilter's outraged shouting and her husband's placatory, "Now Dear, calm down, Dear."

Macklin wished he could take time away from Belmont to go over and tell Elona what he thought of her.

Dr. Pope had, of course, been invited to the party. He ran to Belmont and dropped to his knees beside him. The bullet had hit Belmont in the right lung. The doctor shouted, "Clara, go to my office and get my bag. I need several men here to get this man up off the floor."

Johnny Belmont's face was gray, his lips almost white. As the men started to lift him, he asked Macklin in a weak voice, "Is Doyle dead?"

"Yes."

"You're the marshal now."

"No," said Macklin, "no, Johnny, get someone else."

Belmont shook his head. "You're the marshal now. Get yourself sworn in." Then he added, "Frank Doyle has a brother. Name is Cliff. Big man. Watch out for him. You can handle this. Nobody else in town could. Sorry, Dave."

CHAPTER 2

Dave Macklin was a man who was accustomed to hard physical work, and being the marshal of Contention City was a new kind of experience for him—and not one he enjoyed. Contention was not as wild a town as Tombstone, but the men who worked and lived here were rough and hardworking men, many of them far away from their families, and they drank and gambled and fought because they had nothing else to do when they were off work. And even hardworking, law-abiding men can get out of hand when they are drunk and lonely. Macklin was, for the most part, kept quite busy.

He was anxious for Belmont to get well. Anxious to get back to his life. He felt a compelling need to be building his future, and this temporary job was keeping him from that. He carried within him a constant sense of anxiety, feeling that important time was being irretrievably lost.

As often as he could, he stopped in to visit Johnny Belmont, who had been taken to Dr. Pope's place. They had put him in the back room, the front one being occupied by Clara's patient. Belmont had had a very rough time the first couple of weeks after being shot, and, in fact, it was not until nearly two weeks had passed that the doctor would finally say he was probably going to pull through— adding that it would be many weeks before he'd be able to go back to work.

Macklin spoke to the town council about hiring a deputy but was told there was not enough money in the town's coffers for that luxury. He spoke to them about finding a different replacement for Belmont but was told there was no one willing to do the job— everyone seemed to be worried about what Cliff Doyle would do in retribution for his brother's killing.

Macklin spoke to Johnny Belmont about this, and Belmont said, "You're the man for the job, Dave. You're the one I want in my place, and you're broke. Ain't it kind of nice to have a regular income?"

Grudgingly, Macklin had to concede that point. This single aspect of the job was a positive one.

One morning, while walking up the street toward the office, he saw Herman Chilter shouting at Todd and Mandy Carlson and shooing them away from the butcher shop. Chilter was a short, heavyset man with a round, balding head and a florid complexion. He was jocular and easygoing and was as well liked in town as his wife, Elona, was disliked.

Macklin had never brought up the subject of the six bits he had given the two children to make up for the butcher's unfulfilled part of their bargain, but now, seeing what appeared to be a repeat of the injustice, he strode up to the butcher shop and said in a stern voice, "Herman, I don't think you're being fair with those children."

"What are you talking about, Dave?"

"When you tell them you'll pay them for doing something and they do it, you ought to pay them."

Manifestly affronted by this, the butcher put his hands on his hips and said, "Are you saying I've cheated them?"

"On the day of Sally Pennington's party, I gave those kids the six bits you promised them for rounding up your livestock."

Chilter was pensive for a moment and said, "The day of Sally's party, yes." His red, round face broke into a broad smile and then he laughed out loud. "Were they sitting over there by the horse trough, looking sad?"

Macklin frowned, "Yes."

"Dave, you got took by two of the best sharpers around."

Macklin scowled. The butcher laughed again and said, "Don't feel bad, I got took twice, along with several other people in town."

"Are you going to tell me what you're talking about, or are you just going to stand there laughin' at me all day?"

Chilter said, "The first time my livestock got out, I gave those two kids six bits to round 'em up. The second time, same thing. Third time, I got suspicious. I paid the Adler kid to sleep in my loft and keep an eye on the livestock. Well, just like I suspected, Mandy and Todd were the ones who were busting down the fence and letting the livestock out. So the third time, I went ahead and let them round them up for me before I told them I was onto them. That time I didn't give 'em a red cent."

Feeling completely foolish, Macklin said, "What was it about this time?"

"Well, you know I sell milk here. I have a cow and I milk her, and there are a few people around town who keep a cow and don't drink all the milk she gives, so they bring it to me, and I buy it from them and sell it at a profit to folks who don't have a cow."

"Uh huh," said Macklin. These were things he already knew.

"Well, those two little sharpers were over at Marks' store one day, looking at the Granger's catalogue, and they heard Elona complaining to somebody that I'm so busy with the business of the butcher shop it's hard to find the time to milk my cow twice a day. What they proposed just now is that they milk her for me and I pay them by the gallon."

"What's wrong with that deal?" asked Macklin. "Sounds to me like everybody benefits from it."

"I just don't trust the two little scoundrels. Old man Carlson ought to take a strap to those two instead of just lettin' them run wild the way they do." He paused and chuckled and said, "I'll say one thing, though, for that little gal, Mandy: she watches out for her little brother. One day I saw the Adler kid push the boy down and Mandy flew at him like a fightin' rooster. That poor kid didn't have a chance."

"He's got to be at least two years older than her," observed Macklin.

"Older and bigger; she's twelve and he's fourteen and that didn't help him a bit. Three or four seconds of that little tornado was enough for him. He ran like a scalded dog."

Macklin laughed as he visualized the scene. He knew the Adler kid to be a bully. He said, "Herman, those kids could probably use a little extra money. It's a sure bet their grandpa doesn't give them any. And it would teach them some responsibility. I'll personally stand good for them if anything goes wrong."

Chilter looked at the floor for a long moment and finally said, "All right, Dave. If you see them send 'em over. I'll give 'em a chance."

"Thanks."

Then, acting a little uneasy, Chilter said, "Dave, there's another thing I've been meaning to talk to you about. Fact is, Elona wants me to talk to you about it. She's pretty mad at you."

Macklin waited.

"It's about the night of the party. I wasn't in the room when it happened, but Elona told me you hit her in the chest. I guess you must have, because she had bruises on . . . he reddened . . . "Well, she had bruises. She feels like . . . and I do too, we feel like you owe her an apology."

Macklin was astonished. The woman had touched the match to the powder keg that had killed two men and almost a third—had nearly gotten herself shot in the process—and she wanted an apology. It took him a moment to pull his thoughts together, but when he did, he said, "Herman, tell her she needs to come to me herself with this."

Macklin turned and walked away.

"The Apaches are out, Nan, and I insist you stay here until it's safe to travel," said Nan's mother. Ora White was the antithesis of her sister, Sally. While Sally was short and round, Ora was four inches taller and slender. Nan had inherited her mother's height, but her father's dark hair. Nan's father had died several years before, and Nan, her older sister, and their mother had lived together in Tucson until the death of Sally's husband, when Sally had prevailed upon Ora to come live with her. Around that same time, Nan's sister, Beth, had married, and her husband had come to live with his wife's family. Since that time, Nan had divided her time between the family home in Tucson and Sally's home in Contention City. Of the two, she felt more at home in Sally's.

Ora said, "Beth can get by until it's safe to travel. Then we'll both go and take care of her until the baby comes."

"I don't know," said Nan, struggling with her indecision, "I do hate to impose so long on Aunt Sally's hospitality."

"Impose?" said Sally scornfully, "How could you possibly impose with so many empty rooms in this house? And you're the best singing partner around. Your mother couldn't carry a tune in a potato sack."

Ora laughed. "It's true."

"Believe me," said Sally, "I'm being completely selfish in wanting you to stay. Anyway, Nan, I'm determined to get you married to the right man. I'm very good at matchmaking, you know. There are people who have a gift of spotting two people who are meant to be together, and I'm one of them."

Nan looked at her aunt with raised eyebrows. "You mean that don't you?"

"Oh yes, I'm being very serious."

"You amaze me, Aunt Sally."

"I amaze a lot of people at times. You know, I knew the first time I laid eyes on Arthur that he was the man I would marry . . . and, frankly, I wasn't terribly happy about it at the time."

"Why was that?"

"Well, I was a girl with plenty of romantic notions. I had envisioned myself marrying a tall, handsome fellow, a man of wealth and status. Arthur was none of those. He did later become wealthy, but that was mostly through my motivation and guidance."

Nan grew sober. "Do you miss him terribly?"

"Not always. Most times I just miss him. But yes, sometimes, especially when I'm alone at night, I miss him terribly. Music is what helps me at those times. Now do you understand why I don't want you to go back to Tucson?"

Nan's mother said, "Dear, it would be foolish to travel right now. I know you worry about your sister, and I do too, but in her last letter she said she is doing just fine, and there are other women there who can help until we can get there."

"All right," said Nan, "I'll stay a while longer."

"Good," said Sally. "Now, we'll have tea."

She started to stand up, but Nan took hold of her hand and said, "Not so fast, Aunt Sally. I don't think we've finished our conversation."

"Ah, you want me to tell you if I have discovered who is to be your husband."

"I think it would be only fair."

"I won't. These things are best left to the older and more experienced. They are not things a young girl like you should be meddling in."

Nan and her mother both laughed aloud.

"You are a treasure, Aunt Sally," said Nan. "You've decided who I'm to marry and probably already have a plan to make it happen, and you warn me against meddling."

Sally smiled condescendingly. "We'll have our tea now."

Night after night, Clara sat with her patient. His identity was unknown to them, and, having no other name by which to call him, the doctor and his wife simply referred to him as Clara's patient.

Clara had no doubt she was the reason her patient was still alive. When she sat beside him holding his hand, stroking it and speaking quietly, sometimes reading aloud or softly singing, her patient seemed to rest easy. At these times, his breathing, though shallow, was even and regular; his pulse, though weak, had a regular rate and rhythm. But whenever she left his side these signs of vital normalcy became altered.

One day, Doctor Pope, after checking the patient, asked Clara to follow him to another room. He said, "Clara, I admire what you're doing, but there is a danger. You know what I'm talking about."

Clara knew to what the doctor was referring, but she pretended not to. "No, John, what is the danger you're talking about?"

He could tell by her tone and the set of her jaw that it would be unwise to carry this subject any further, so he merely said, "Just be careful, Clara, that's all I'm saying. We don't know anything about this man."

The Apaches attacked at dawn, seemingly coming out of nowhere. Within a few minutes every man and mule in the train of freight wagons was dead, and by the time twenty more minutes had passed, the Apaches had torn through the goods in the wagons, taken what they wanted, and set the rest afire. Alerted by the smoke, the army patrol—led by Captain Paul Bitner—arrived to find dead men, dead mules, ashes, and little else.

"Let's get them buried, Sergeant," said Bitner grimly

Sergeant Gately, a big Irishman, swung out of the saddle and began bellowing orders.

After the bodies were buried, Sergeant Gately said, "It was the guns they were after, Sor, and their ammunition."

"Well, they got them, Sergeant."

"Yes Sor, they did."

"Mount up," said Bitner in a subdued tone.

Gately repeated the phrase for all to hear.

The detail rode to town, a mild, following breeze keeping them in the very center of their own cloud of dust. When they arrived, the men and horses were the color of the desert.

Dismounting in front of the marshal's office, Bitner said to Gately, "We'll stay two hours." He walked inside, leaving Gately behind him barking orders.

Dave Macklin was sitting at the desk doing paper work, a thing he detested. He looked up, and without smiling, said, "Captain Bitner."

Bitner was a tall man; good looking and vain because of it, he could never pass a mirror without at least stealing a glance at his reflection. He was a good soldier, however, and had risen to his current rank through his own merit.

He began beating the dust off his clothes with his hat, and Macklin said, "You could have done that outside."

Bitner pointedly looked around the shabby office with its unplastered adobe walls and said, "Does it matter?"

Angling his head toward a chair by way of invitation, Macklin said, "What can I do for you, Captain?"

Bitner took a seat. "Aw, Dave, we used to be better friends than that. Have you forgotten?"

Macklin opened the desk drawer and withdrew two glasses, which he poured a quarter full. "How could I, Captain?"

"You're a civilian now, Dave. There's no regulation that says you have to address me by my rank. We used to use each other's first names."

Macklin took a sip of whiskey. "Why don't you come to the point? You wouldn't be here without a reason."

Bitner looked down at his drink, swirling it in the glass for a few moments. Inside the room there was only silence. "Would it make any difference if I told you I'm sorry? That I was wrong?"

"It might if I thought you really meant it. But you don't. You just want something. What is it?"

Paul Bitner produced two cigars and handed one to Macklin, and the two men spent a few moments lighting them and inhaling the fragrant smoke. Presently Bitner said, "I need you back. It's as simple as that. But not as an officer. I need a scout who really knows the Apache."

"What about your Apache scouts?"

"There are some good ones, but I can't get them. The ones I've been given are . . . Let's just say, they seem to be on the side of the enemy."

"Understandable."

"The Apaches I'm hunting are running me all over the country, wearing out my men and my horses, laughing at the cavalry. As far as I know, I haven't come within twenty miles of them."

"I have," said Macklin.

"Yeah, I heard about that. You were lucky." He paused and said, "But then, you've always been lucky."

"Except in love."

Bitner winced and looked away for a moment. Turning back to Macklin, he said, "Well, what do you say?"

"No."

Bitner frowned. "If it were any other officer asking you to do this, you'd do it. But because it's me . . ." There was a long pause, and he said, "You were always a good man, Dave, but you've always had a hard time forgiving."

"That's just the way it is, Captain."

Bitner finished his drink and said, "We were a lot younger then, Dave, we . . ." He looked away and continued speaking as though to someone not present. "She wasn't what we thought she was. She didn't deserve you. You were the lucky one."

"That's not the point."

Bitner swung his head back, "I know what the point is. I know very well, but you need to understand something. I learned a few things from that experience. And I got paid back ten times over for what I did. I don't know what a man has to do—"

"Forget it," broke in Macklin. "It's in the past."

"Not for you, Dave. That's the problem." Bitner rose and turned toward the door. Walking away, he said, "The offer stands."

When Bitner was gone, Macklin sat for a time, idly smoking his cigar and sipping his drink, thinking, remembering. Bitner was right about one thing, he knew: He had a hard time forgiving. He had always been that way. He had never viewed it as a character flaw until now. He had always told himself it was a defensive trait that saved him from being worked over a second time by the same person.

But Bitner had put things in a different light, and, try though he might, Macklin could not dispel the thought that maybe, of the two of them, Paul Bitner, the man he detested, was the better man. He rose from his chair, downed the last of his drink, and stepped out into the brilliant light of the day.

⁓⤳⤳⤳⁓

"Come on," said Mandy, "Hurry up."

"Why?" asked Todd. "Why do we have to go every night?"

"Because," was all she answered.

They took off their shoes, and in the darkness they waded the shallow San Pedro at a wide spot. Half a mile downstream was the bridge, but Mandy was in a hurry. With their shoes and socks back on, she threaded a path through the catclaw and creosote bush, carefully skirting a thicket of jumping cactus, and led the way to the large house on the side of the hill.

At a particular spot, just outside the rectangle of light that shone out of a window in Sally Pennington's music room, they sat in their usual place and waited. It was not a long wait, for Sally Pennington was a creature of habit and Mandy knew her schedule.

Carrying a lamp, one of the servants entered the room and lit the bracket lamps on the walls, afterward opening the window. Not thirty seconds later, Sally Pennington entered, followed by Nan, who sat at the piano and played a scale to limber up her fingers.

When Nan stopped playing, Sally placed a sheet of music in front of her and said, "Let's start with this one."

For over an hour, the two women sang while Nan played accompaniment, their voices blending beautifully. Nan was an accomplished pianist and a talented singer, and her aunt Sally was a former opera singer. Several of Sally's servants came in and sat to listen, for Sally was no martinet, and she liked an audience, however small it may be.

The servants enjoyed the nightly concert a great deal, but the most enrapt of all the spectators was unseen, hidden in the darkness outside the window, sitting on the ground next to her sleeping brother.

~~~

It was nearly sundown when Cliff Doyle and six of his riders rode up to within a hundred feet of the house and hailed it.

"Hello the house," yelled Doyle.

Doyle knew he and his men were being observed by unseen watchers, and he wanted to make it clear this was not a hostile visit.

A burly, dirty-looking man wearing a yellow shirt stepped out onto the front porch of the house, where he stood holding a rifle, mutely looking at the Double H riders.

"We come to talk," said Doyle.

"Then do it."

"I'd rather come in and sit down, maybe have a smoke."

Motioning with his head, the yellow-shirted man said, "Just you, not them."

Doyle dismounted and handed the reins to one of his men. Inside the house, the yellow-shirted man motioned Doyle to a chair in front of a deal table, and both men sat.

Doyle said, "Name's Cliff Doyle. Good to meet you."

The yellow-shirted man said nothing. Men began filtering back into the house from outside. There was a woman in another room, cooking.

Doyle looked around at the men in the room and said, "Is there any place where we can talk?"

The yellow-shirted man swung his head toward his men and growled, "Get out."

When they were alone, Doyle came to the point, "I figure we ought to work together."

"What makes you figure that?"

"You're a business man, so am I," said Doyle with a meaningful smile. "Sometimes a man who runs cows—purely by accident, mind you—finds himself with some cattle on his hands with brands that . . . ain't quite usual."

"Is that what got you run out of Texas."

"A hop and a skip ahead of a fifty-man posse," said Doyle, who, far from being embarrassed or ashamed, seemed proud of the fact. He continued, "Me and my brother, we saw it comin', sent some boys ahead with a herd. That's how we got our start here in Arizona."

"Get to the point."

"Point is we can work together. Me and my men will get the cattle, and we'll change or vent the brands. You find the buyer for 'em, and we split the profits. There's hundreds of thousands of acres of range land in this territory, cattle scattered all over it. Not enough riders watchin' over 'em to count for anything."

Doyle had not come to this meeting blind. He knew these were outlaws and that they sometimes rustled cattle, drove them north, and came back without them. This meant they had a buyer. And he, Doyle, did not. And, being new to the area, he had been unable to find one.

"What's the split?" asked the yellow-shirted man.

"Sixty-forty."

"Who gets sixty?"

"Why, I would," answered Doyle.

The outlaw stood up. "Fifty-fifty, or you can ride out of here right now."

Doyle made a show of contemplating this, then grinned. "Fine." He extended his hand and said, "Like I said, my name's Cliff Doyle."

"Ben Lukert," said the yellow-shirted man, accepting the hand.

There was a bottle of whiskey on the table. Doyle eyed it and Lukert said, "Go ahead."

Doyle looked around for a glass, but there were none, so he guessed these men didn't use them. He took a deep swig.

Ben Lukert was not going into this arrangement blind either. He knew who Doyle was, knew where his spread was, had even rustled a few head of cattle from him. He said, "Heard about your brother. Too bad."

Doyle's eyes hardened. "He was a fool goin' in there the way he did."

The outlaw nodded his agreement.

Then Doyle said, "Back in Texas, people knew somethin' about us Doyles. You picked a fight with one of us, you was pickin' a fight with all of us. The man that killed a Doyle had to die."

Which one of them marshals killed your brother? The old one or the new one?"

"Don't know. Floyd said things happened so fast he wasn't sure who shot who."

"And so?" queried Lukert.

"Don't matter none," said Doyle. "I'll kill 'em both."

An ugly smile creased Ben Lukert's face. "You and me, we think alike."

"Clara, you've performed a miracle. He's still alive, and I figure if he hasn't died by now he's out of immediate danger. But you know, he may never come out of this coma."

Clara looked down at her patient with a certain fondness and said, "I think he will, Doctor. Somehow I think he will."

Two days later, a cowboy knocked at their front door and was invited in. "I better not come in, Doc, or I'll get blood all over your rug." He pointed to his booted foot and the doctor saw that part the boot was missing and blood was issuing from it.

"Did you shoot yourself in the foot, Doug?"

"I did, Doc."

"How did you manage that? Clara, bring me some clean cloths."

Looking chagrined, Doug said, "I was practicin' my quick draw."

"Well, you've shot off your big toe," said the doctor after a quick examination.

Doug swore. "That's kind of what it felt like, Doc. I ruined my boot, too."

"I've got to sew this thing up, Doug."

"You fix boots, too?"

"Your toe, Doug, I've got to sew up your toe—and it's not going to feel good."

A short time later, Doug's howling could be heard outside the doctor's house and down the street.

It was at this moment that Clara's patient opened his eyes.

Macklin checked on Johnny Belmont's progress every day, at times going over in the evening as well, sometimes staying long enough to play a game or two of checkers. The marshal's color was getting better and he was starting to put on some of the weight he had lost.

During one of these visits, the doctor came in and said to Macklin, "If you're tired of being marshal, it shouldn't be too much longer. I'd say another week and we'll throw him out of here. After that, if he still doesn't want to work, you can arrest him for vagrancy."

Macklin received this news with mixed emotions. He didn't want to be the marshal of Contention City forever, but on the other hand, he wasn't sure what he was going to do when he no longer had the job. He had wanted to be a rancher and had been doing well until the Apaches had stolen his horses.

Five days later, Paul Bitner rode into town at the head of a dusty, thirsty detail of men, all of them grim-faced and solemn.

"Sergeant, see that the horses are taken care of. We'll be pulling out in two hours." He went directly to the marshal's office, and not finding Macklin there, he found Macklin's whisky and a glass in the desk drawer and poured some for himself. He was sitting in a chair drinking it when Macklin arrived.

"Hello, Captain," said Macklin, without inflection.

Bitner gave the tiniest of nods. "Dave."

"What can I do for you?"

Bitner produced a small bundle he had been holding on his lap, set it on the desk, and unwrapped it. It was a woman's bonnet and a child's rag doll. Both of them were stained with blood, and Macklin understood the grimness on the soldier's countenance.

Bitner spoke. "Dave, you and I have had our problems. You hate my guts and maybe you always will, but I can't tell you how little that kind of thing matters after you've seen what I've seen today."

"Who?" said Macklin.

"The Blakes and the Nielsons. Every man, woman, and child. He poured himself another drink and gulped a mouthful of it. Macklin could see the man was deeply affected by what he had seen. Macklin himself was deeply affected by the news. He had known the two families. Had eaten at their tables. He remained silent, unable to think of anything to say.

Presently Bitner broke the silence. "I need you to be my scout, Dave. You know the Apaches, you know their ways, you know the country. You're the best tracker I've ever known." He pointed to the bloody objects sitting on the desk. "If you say no, there'll be more of these and they'll be on your conscience."

Macklin pulled his eyes away from the doll and the bonnet. "I'll need to go tell Johnny he's lost his replacement."

⌣⌣⌣

Big drops of sweat fell from Dave Macklin's face onto the tracks he was studying, and he took off his hat and mopped his brow with his bandana. He said to the big Irishman who was squatting beside him on the trail, "What do you think the temperature is today, Sergeant?"

"It'll be a hundred and fifteen if it's a degree," responded Gately.

Macklin moved to another set of tracks, walking alongside them and bent over, scanning the ground. Without looking at Gately, he said, "And what do you think the temperature is today in Ireland?"

"Ah, now you wouldn't be makin' an Irishman think of home on a day like today, would you Sor?"

Straightening and turning to speak to Bitner, who sat astride his horse nearby, Macklin said, "You're wrong Captain, There's more of them than you think, and it looks to me like they're running in three groups. But sometimes they come back together. They're doing it to confuse us."

"Well, it worked," said Bitner bitterly. Then, as Macklin mounted his horse, Bitner said, "What do you suggest we do now?"

"I think . . ." said Macklin. His voice fell off as he scanned the surrounding desert, his eyes attempting to pierce the undulating heat waves that rose up from its surface. Finally, he said, "I think we do our very best to keep from being drawn into a trap, because that's what they're trying to do."

He turned to Bitner. "One group would get us to follow them to a place they had already picked for an ambush. Another group would meet them there and they would hit us from two sides and the front while the third group came up behind and hit us from the rear. It would be a bloody massacre."

"Why do you suppose," queried Bitner, "they haven't done it before now?"

"Who knows? They're Apaches. Only Apaches know why they do what they do. But I'd say you've been pretty lucky."

"It occurs to me, Sor, if you don't mind me speaking out of turn," said Gately, "every place they've hit they've been takin' guns and ammunition. Maybe they didn't have enough. Maybe they were gatherin' up weaponry so that every man of them would have somethin' to shoot at us with."

Bitner nodded contemplatively. "What do you think, Dave?"

"Probably."

There was a long silence as the three men pondered this information. Bitner broke the silence, saying, "The only way to avoid being lured into a trap is not to follow any group of Apaches. And yet we're out here to capture or kill them. How do we do that if we don't follow them?"

Macklin did not directly answer the question. He said, "We need more men."

"We don't have more men."

"Then you'll have to take some risks."

"Such as?"

"We have to beat them at their own game," said Macklin. "Picking up the trail of a group of them and following is never going to work. Even if they didn't lure us into an ambush, they'd always keep ahead of us. They'd always know what we were going to do the minute we started doing it."

"So what do you propose?"

"Give me two volunteers. Give us supplies and water and the three best horses you've got. We'll move out in the middle of the night. You'll meet us back here five days from now. We'll do some scouting meanwhile."

It took a long time for Bitner to make his decision. He knew it would be very dangerous for the three men, but he also knew something different had to be tried. A large group of mounted soldiers could never keep its whereabouts unknown to the Apaches. The dust of their passage could be seen for miles.

"Well Dave, I've trusted you before. I guess I'll trust you now. Five days."

Riding away at the head of the column, Paul Bitner turned in the saddle and watched as Macklin, Gately, and Johnson disappeared into the murky night. He hoped he had made the right decision, but right or wrong, he had a sense of dissatisfaction with himself and he quickly identified its source: Why would men like Gately and Johnson, the two best men in the troop, so quickly volunteer to go with Macklin on such a dangerous mission? He knew what it was, and he tried to suppress the jealousy he felt. He had felt that jealousy before. There was a quality that Macklin possessed that Bitner recognized to be lacking in himself. He was a good officer as far as it went, but men followed him mostly because he was their superior and it was their duty.

With Macklin it was different. He inspired in men a kind of respect and trust that made them want to follow him. This was a trait of which Bitner was convinced Macklin was unaware.

He recalled bitterly a conversation he had accidentally overheard between two of his superior officers. It had taken place at a get-together at a fellow officer's house in the time when Bitner and Macklin were still the best of friends—two young lieutenants with their careers ahead of them.

The two senior officers were discussing Bitner's qualities as an officer, and the conversation eventually turned to one in which his more human traits were discussed. "Well, he certainly loves women," commented the first officer, to which the second—a much older man—replied, "No, he likes women. He does not love them, nor does he respect them. A man who loves women respects them and treats them with the deference a respectable woman deserves. That's one of the many differences between Bitner and Macklin."

"They are both interested in the same woman," observed the first officer.

"You are referring to Marie Latham."

"Yes."

"And she is not deserving of either of them. And mark my words, she will destroy their friendship before it's all over."

Bitner had left the party and tried to tell himself the comments were not true. He had tried to forget them, but now their sting was revived by the fact that the older officer's words had proven so prophetic. This, combined with the jealousy Bitner was feeling right now, diminished him in his own eyes. Just for a moment, he found himself hoping Dave Macklin would not return from this dangerous mission. The thought jolted him, and he raised his hand, reined in his horse, and sat there for a moment with the calm and curious troopers waiting behind him.

He thought of going back. There was still time to recall the three men and tell them he had changed his mind. But it was a good plan and he knew it. It would be wrong to allow personal feelings to enter into it. Macklin had volunteered, and so had the other two men, and one thing Bitner could say to himself with complete honesty was that when he had agreed to the plan it had been because he had believed it was the right way to proceed. His motives had been purely professional.

The column pushed on, enveloped in dust, and after a while, Bitner's thoughts turned to more pleasant things. He looked forward with great anticipation to the party Sally Pennington was hosting in two days.

Bitner's mother had been a friend of the Pennington family back in Baltimore, and it was because of this connection that Bitner had gone to Sally Pennington's home one day to pay his respects to her. She had been delighted to see him and had extended a standing invitation to all her parties. It was at one of those parties that he had met Nan White.

Bitner was an ambitious man. He was determined to rise in rank and one day be a general. In order to do that, an army man needed a wife. And an attractive, charming wife was the best kind. Many times, Bitner had observed what an asset an officer's wife could be to his career if she was the right kind of woman, and he had often observed with wonder and disdain the homely or timid women some military men chose to marry. He had promised himself he would not make that mistake.

The first time he had met Nan, he had known she would be the perfect officer's wife, and he had decided then and there to marry her.

Dr. Pope stood looking down at Clara's patient with intense interest. One of his eyes seemed to be clear and focused. The other did not. There was brain damage, and it was certainly not unexpected.

"What's your name?" he asked the patient.

The patient's lips parted and closed again several times, but no words came out. After a few tries, he gave up and closed his eyes, exhausted by the effort.

Clara turned to the doctor, tears glistening in her eyes, and whispered, "He woke up."

The doctor turned and beckoned her to follow him. In another room he said, "Do not expect too much, Clara. The fact that he can't speak is not a good sign."

"But it's early," she said.

"Maybe so, but don't get your hopes too high. Did you notice that when he tried to move his mouth one side of his face was not moving?"

"No," she lied.

"That's partial paralysis. We don't know how far that extends. It could extend to the entire left side of his body. And what if he's lost his memory? He could be like a small child, not knowing how to speak or walk . . . not remembering anything."

Clara looked at the floor, saying nothing, and Doctor Pope watched her face for a few moments. Presently she said, "He has a nice face, don't you think? He must be a good man."

The doctor had no notion of whether or not Clara's patient was a good man, and he didn't care about the man's face. He did, however, worry about Clara's emotional attachment to this patient. In an attempt to make her confront what he saw as a very cruel possibility, he said, "Let's hope he remembers who he is so we can notify his wife and family."

After leaving Bitner's detail, Macklin and his two volunteer companions, Sergeant Gately and Trooper Johnson, rode to the scene of the last known massacre: the small valley where the Blake and Nielson families had made their homes. Everything was as the Apaches had left it, except for the row of wooden crosses standing on a rise behind one of the houses. Macklin struggled to keep his mind away from what those crosses represented. He tried not to remember faces. These people had been his friends.

The Apaches must have been in a hurry, he thought. Having killed everyone here, it appeared they had left quickly, taking only the weapons and ammunition they found. He believed Gately to be right: The Apaches were amassing firearms and ammunition.

There were a few items scattered on the ground around the houses and more on the floors inside. The houses were made of stone, so only their roofs and contents would have burned. Perhaps, thought Macklin, it was for this reason the Apaches had not seen the point in setting fire to the places. Or maybe they had not wanted to make any smoke to advertise their whereabouts.

They picked up the trail of the band of Indians that had perpetrated the massacre and began following, moving slowly in order to spare their mounts in the murderous heat and to avoid raising any more dust than necessary.

After a few miles, it was clear to Macklin that the Apaches had made no effort to hide their trail. This, Macklin knew, meant that either they had no fear of the cavalry following them, or they wanted to be followed. Either way, he knew the Indians would have been carefully watching their back trail, and he was glad it was now two days old.

Even so, it would not do to get careless.

Macklin knew this desert probably as well as any white man, but the Apaches knew it better. And hardy as they and their ponies were, they could not survive without water. So, he trusted the trail would lead to water sooner or later.

The following day, it did. Hidden among the rocks at the base of the mountain was a small seep that came up out of the ground as if by magic. There it formed a tiny pool which overflowed and followed a narrow stream bed, soon losing itself in the thirsty desert earth.

The men partook of the tepid water and afterward let the horses drink. Johnson and Gately wanted to make camp next to the seep that night, but Macklin said, "There aren't many water holes in this desert. You never know who might show up in the middle of the night. And I don't think it would be white men."

They left the trail they had been following and rode a couple of miles away to a deep-cut wash where they made a cold camp—if anything could be called cold in the Arizona desert this time of year. There was a small meadow nearby with some grass that still retained a little green from the last rain, and there they picketed the horses.

After a meager meal of jerky, hard tack, and biscuit, washed down by canteen water, the three men lay back against the sloping side of the wash and gazed up at the stars, each with his own thoughts. This was the time when a man would have a smoke and think about home and loved ones, but Macklin permitted no smoking, knowing the smell of tobacco could carry far on the clean desert air.

Presently he said to Gately, "How long have we known each other?"

"Eight, maybe ten years, I'm thinkin', Captain."

"You don't have to call me Captain any more, Sergeant. I'm just a scout now."

"That's true, Captain, but I like the sound of it, if you don't mind."

Macklin said, "You've never told me what brought an Irishman like yourself to this desert."

"I came to help fight the war between the states," said Gately, "like so many other Irishmen."

Macklin had expected this answer. He had known a good many Irishmen who had come for the war and stayed in the army afterward. And he was glad to have one of them along with him on this mission.

Gately continued, "And the war ended, as you know yourself, so I went to work takin' care of a rich man's hawrses back in Washington. But, somehow the job didn't suit me."

"Why?" asked Johnson.

"I suppose I was too restless. And the job was too tame. I felt somethin' pullin' me to the west, so I went and got a job helpin' to build the railroad, drivin' spikes all across the plains. Now, that, M'lads, is a job for an Irishman."

"Or a Chinaman," jibed Johnson.

Gately ignored the jibe. "And then one day I woke up drunk and broke and decided I'd best join the army again before I starved to death. The army's been good to me. It's not an easy life, but it has its merits, and it's a job that'll never go away. I was there when that last spike was driven and we were all paid off and sent on our way, jobless. We had finished a task and it was a good feelin', I'll not deny it, but I decided I wanted a job that would have no end. It came into my head that the job of men killin' each other has been goin' on since Cain did Abel.

"There'll never be an end to armies, and there'll never be an end to wars. There'll never be a day when the last bullet is fired or the last man falls dead from it. Soldiers will always have work to do until the good Lard decides He's had enough and comes to clean His house. And I suppose I'll be dead and gone before that day comes."

"That sheds a pretty sorry light on the human race," commented Johnson.

"Any race that devotes as much time and effort as we do toward killin' itself off is a pretty sorry thing," agreed Gately.

"How about you, Johnson?" asked Macklin. "What brought you out here?"

"Me?" Johnson hesitated. "Well, back where I'm from, I'm wanted for murder."

"Well, now that's quite a thing to be tellin' your ridin' companions at a time like this," said Gately.

Johnson chuckled. "It was a big mistake. A rich man accused me of getting too familiar with his wife. He tried to horsewhip me, and we fought. He pulled a gun, and I had to defend myself. His brother claimed to have seen the whole thing. He said it was murder. It was a lie: He was nowhere near at the time, but he was a rich man and I wasn't."

"The rich man's lie always carries more weight than the poor man's truth," observed Gately.

Withdrawing from the discussion, Macklin leaned his head back and closed his eyes, attempting to think of thoughts more cheering than man's inhumanity to man. Automatically he thought of Nan White. He remembered her tall, slender form gliding gracefully across the room at Sally Pennington's party. He remembered her face as it had looked when she sat across from him. He had not understood the way she looked at him. Had that been genuine interest in her eyes, or was she merely being polite? He had hoped to get to know her better that night, to converse longer with her and perhaps take a stroll with her out in Sally's garden, but the gunfight with Doyle and his men had put an end to that possibility.

A pretty woman could always have her choice of men. There were plenty of men who looked no deeper than that, and Macklin had promised himself he would not make that mistake again. He felt certain it was not just Nan White's beauty that had attracted him to her, but something about her that bespoke goodness and kindness. Sally Pennington had a great fondness for her, and Sally Pennington was one of the best judges of character Macklin had ever known.

He became suddenly aware of the deep breathing of his two companions and realized they were asleep. Remembering he had assigned the first watch to himself, he got up and found a good spot for it and spent the next two hours forcing his mind to stay awake and alert.

Mandy sat on a rock and dangled her feet in the cool, shallow water of the San Pedro river while her brother added water to the milk in the pails. She looked at the open page of the atlas she held on her lap, the one she had brazenly borrowed from Mrs. Marks, and then shifted her gaze to the river. It was true then: The San Pedro flowed from south to north. The Atlas said it began down in Mexico and flowed up through Arizona to where it converged with another river.

But how could that be? According to the atlas, north was at the top of the globe and south was at the bottom, which meant the San Pedro was flowing uphill. She wished there were someone she could ask—someone who would be kind and not put her off or ridicule her. Someone with sufficient education to answer her questions with valid information. It never occurred to her to ask her grandfather. He was a millworker and worked long hours, and when he was home, he drank. He was a likeable man when he was sober, but he was rarely sober, and when he was, Mandy didn't feel comfortable asking him questions.

Her older sister, Lena, was kind and intelligent but had received very little education, and she was rarely able to answer Mandy's questions.

"Ready," said Todd.

They picked up their pails of watered-down milk and carried them to the butcher shop, where they would sell them to Herman Chilter for the usual price.

***

Awakened by the heat of the morning sun, Sergeant Gately opened his eyes and quickly took stock of his surroundings. Two hours of sleep had left him groggy and lethargic. Johnson, sitting nearby, extended a piece of jerky to him and said, "Breakfast."

They sat chewing the jerky for a while, and Gately said, "I don't like him goin' off alone like that."

Johnson shrugged. "Knows what he's doing."

Gately found a small stick and began idly tracing patterns in the sand of the wash bed, where they were planning to remain until nightfall. After a while, the position of the sun drove the shade away from the wash, and the men sat, miserably hot under the beating sun.

Presently there was shade on the opposite side of the wash, and they moved across the wash, flattening their bodies against the steep bank as the shade gradually deepened in the afternoon.

There was a sound above them, and Macklin slid down the bank and deposited himself next to Gately. Without having to be asked, Gately handed him a canteen and he drank deeply and gratefully, afterward accepting a piece of jerky and a biscuit. Having partially sated his thirst and hunger, he laid his head back against the bank and said, "Looks like we were right. There's a large number of them, and I know where their camp is."

"Did you see it?" asked Gately.

"No, I didn't get that close, but I got close enough to smell the fires and I saw a couple of squaws gathering wood. They were a good distance from camp, which means they've used up all the wood nearby. They've been there a while."

"Well, Captain, we've done what we came to do. Now if we can make it to the rendezvous with our hair still in place I think we can call this a successful mission," said Gately.

They spent the remainder of the day resting—sleep was impossible in this heat—and when it was fully dark they set out. They traveled slowly, knowing that even at night—especially at night—an Indian could smell dust in the air from a good distance away. Even so, when morning came, Macklin estimated they had traveled something between fifteen and twenty miles from dusk until dawn. They were tired, and their horses were worn out.

He led them to an old mine he knew of at the base of a mountain. It had been abandoned for many years and was not very deep, but there was a seep of water near it and it was cool enough inside that a man could sleep through the heat of the day if he was tired enough. Not far away was a place where they picketed their horses to graze on the parched grass.

A decaying wooden ladder took them from the surface down about fifteen feet into the man-made cavern where the tunnel straightened and traveled horizontally for another twenty feet or so. They checked it for snakes and, finding it safe, took their bedrolls down. After clearing away some rocks and debris, they rolled their blankets out on the mine floor.

"I'll take the first watch," said Macklin, and he climbed back up the precarious ladder, walked to the nearest hill, and found a good spot on top where he could be concealed while watching the countryside.

Gazing over the land, he asked himself, not for the first time, what it was about this Arizona desert that he loved. He recalled the green of Colorado and Wyoming—places where he had spent some time—the deep-hued grasses and trees, the plentiful streams and creeks and rivers, the frequent rainstorms; all of which, when contrasted with the hostile land he saw before him, dry and hot, studded with barren rocky hills and mountains; made him wonder why any human being would choose to live here. And yet no matter where he went, he was always drawn back. He knew what he felt, but he could never have explained it to another person.

In the distance, he saw a hint of dust in the air. For twenty minutes, he watched until he saw a group of mounted Indians come over a rise in the earth. If they continued in the direction they were going, they would cut the trail he and his companions had made and would surely follow it.

Taking great care not to raise any dust, he made his way down the hill to the mine. Leaning over its rim he spoke to the two men below. "Get up, we've got to get going, now!"

The horses were weary and still hungry. They were not happy about being saddled again. They had been grazing on scanty, half-dry desert grass for the past five days, and Macklin hoped that if it came to a race they would have the stamina to outdistance the Indian ponies.

The men left their bedrolls and supplies—except for their canteens and ammunition—in the mine, knowing their greatest need was haste. With the horses saddled, Macklin climbed the hill again and, peering over its rim, was shocked to see how close the Indians were. And they were definitely following the tracks he and his companions had left on the way to the mine. Then, a show of dust from another direction caught his attention and chilled his heart. He hurried back down the hill to where Gately and Johnson waited with the horses.

He said, "They're coming from two directions. They've almost got us boxed in."

They could not climb the mountain behind them, which left only one direction for them to go. The Indians must know that, too. Were they simply leaving that avenue open, or was it a trap? Macklin wondered. He wasted no time in deliberation. Their only chance lay to the east, and in that direction the three men rode as fast as their weary horses could carry them.

Chapter 3

"**M**ilton," yelled Sally Pennington, "Oh, Milton."

Soon Milton appeared, wearing his usual vapid smile, and stood in the doorway expectantly.

"You can go get the milk now, Milton."

Milton's smile widened. He nodded and turned and, in his odd gait, left the house, running.

Sally turned to Ora and Nan and said, "He does so love to be given something to do, poor boy. It makes him feel important."

"Was he born like that?" asked Nan.

"Oh no, he was a normal child, a beautiful child—my dear husband's favorite nephew. He fell off a barn roof when he was seven years old. Landed on a pile of bricks. His brain was damaged. His father was devastated. His mother had died years before, you know. And then some years later when his father died, Arthur brought him to live with us. He's been with us ever since."

"He seems to have adapted well to Arizona."

"Probably better than I have. When Arthur and I first came out here I was very discouraged. I swore that if I had to stay here six months I would curl up in a ball and die, but I got over that. I can't say I love the desert the way you do, Nan, but I've grown accustomed to it. I've even grown used to the constant noise of the mill. Yes, I guess I have to say this is my home. And here I will stay until the good Lord takes me . . ." she chuckled, "wherever he decides to take me."

It took Milton longer than it would have taken a normal person to go to the butcher shop and get the milk, but as Sally had said, he loved doing it. Though he was almost a middle-aged man, Milton possessed the mind of a child, and the praise Nan and Sally and Ora lavished upon him every time he performed even the smallest task caused him to beam with delight.

Milton returned with the milk. The three women seated themselves at the breakfast table. The food was brought out, along with three large glasses of milk on a tray. Nan took a drink and noticed the milk tasted a little thin but politely refrained from commenting. Sally seemed to be watching her intently. She said, "Put the glass down, Nan. No, give it to me." She held the glass up close to her face and set it down. With an angry set to her jaw, she said, "Anna, tell Edward to come here please."

"What's wrong?" asked Ora.

"Take a close look," said Sally, pointing to the glass of milk.

Ora leaned closer to the glass and suddenly flinched away, "Oh, my," she exclaimed.

When Edward came in, Sally said, "I'll need my carriage, Edward. We are going to town."

When they walked into the butcher shop, Herman Chilter looked up, and seeing Sally Pennington's face, said, "Don't even say it, I already know. You found minnows in your milk."

"I've been thinking it was a little thin for several days now," said Sally, "but I didn't think you would stoop to watering down the milk you sell."

"It wasn't me, Mrs. Pennington. It was those Carlson kids. I've been paying them to milk my cow and theirs. I pay them by the gallon for the milk. Looks like they thought they'd found a way to improve their profits."

Sally and Nan and Ora burst into laughter, but Herman Chilter didn't smile. "I'll return your money," he said to Sally.

"No," said Sally, "I'm not worried about the money. I'm just glad to know you're still an honest businessman." She was silent for a moment, looking pensively down at the counter while she tapped her fingers on it. Then, looking up, she said, "I don't suppose you would be willing to give the two little urchins another chance, would you, if Nan and I spoke to them about the importance of honesty in their business dealings?"

"They've already had their second chance with me," he said, "and I got talked into that against my better judgement."

"By whom?" asked Nan.

"Dave Macklin."

Clara's patient was able to respond to simple questions by nodding his head or moving it from side to side in negation. It was still difficult to tell how well his brain was functioning because to some questions he simply did not reply, and neither Clara nor the doctor could tell for sure if he was unable to respond or simply refused to do so. Clara felt the former was the case, but the doctor disagreed, basing his disagreement on the kinds of questions the patient did not answer.

In one of their frequent discussions about the patient's status he said, "It's always the personal questions he doesn't answer, Clara. Like when you asked him if he knows his name, if he knows where he's from, if he knows who did this to him. He doesn't respond at all to those questions. He doesn't even try."

"He just needs more time."

"Well he's got that," said Doctor Pope. "Until he can get up out of that bed and walk away from here, he's got time."

The people of Contention had come to rely on Sally Pennington's parties as the main form of cultured entertainment in their town, and those parties stood in stark contrast with the raw and raucous offerings of the rougher side of town.

Unlike many army officers who were hard put to scrape by on their meager salaries, Bitner was from a wealthy family and could afford an extra dress uniform designated solely for use at Sally's parties.

It being impossible to ride across the dry Arizona desert without becoming dust-covered, he kept this uniform at Sally's house, where, always arriving before the other guests, he would change into it. The uniform had been specially tailored for him, and, being a good-looking man, he thought he looked quite distinguished in it.

On this particular day, Bitner had arrived earlier than usual, had cleaned up and donned his dress uniform, and was now downstairs waiting for the rest of the guests to arrive so the party could begin.

Nan came out wearing a blue-satin dress and greeted him in a way that neither gave nor dispelled hope. It was the way of women, he thought, to keep a man guessing.

"She's been wanting to go back to Tucson," said Nan's mother. "Talk her out of it, Captain. Tell her how dangerous the trip would be with the Apaches out."

"She's right," said Bitner. "But when the time comes that you simply have to get back to Tucson, the army would be more than happy to escort you."

"Even with an army escort," asserted Ora, "it would still be too dangerous to suit me."

"How long do you think it will be," asked Nan, "before the Apaches are subdued?"

"Well, that's my job," said Bitner, "and so far I haven't been doing it very well. But I have some men out on scout and if they locate the Apache's main camp—and I'm confident they will—I think we'll soon see an end to the problem."

"I understand Mr. Macklin is working for the army now," said Sally. "Will he be joining us tonight?"

"No . . . actually, he's one of the men out on scout right now."

Something subtle crossed Nan's face and Bitner was not sure what it was—but it bothered him.

She said, "That sounds like quite a dangerous mission."

"Oh, I don't know," said Bitner. "Out here a soldier's job is never safe, but I wouldn't say this mission is particularly hazardous."

He appeared somewhat ill at ease, and Sally stepped in smoothly and said, "I'm sure Captain Bitner has been on plenty of hazardous missions himself."

Recognizing what Sally was doing, Nan said, "I have no doubt of it."

Offering her his arm, Bitner said, "Would you like to take a turn in the garden?"

Johnson's horse gave out first, late in the afternoon, and, after stripping off the saddle and bridle, they left it where it had dropped. Macklin had had the best horse to begin with, and Johnson climbed up behind him. Neither of the two remaining mounts would last much longer and the men knew it. Whatever hope they had depended on them getting to a place Macklin knew of. A place he knew as a highly defensible position.

But after less than two miles, Macklin dismounted and said, "Get down, Boys, these horses are finished. We can make better time on foot."

There had been no sign of the Indians for miles, and the men had no way of knowing how close they were. Leading their mounts, they made it without incident to the spot Macklin was aiming for, and there they unsaddled the horses and left them in a small, shallow valley where there was a little graze but, unfortunately, no water. They didn't bother picketing the animals, knowing that in their condition they would not have the strength to wander.

The three men had no supplies other than what few they had carried in their saddlebags, but they had had the foresight to bring their ammunition. And when they climbed the steep slope to the spot Macklin had chosen to defend, Gately said, "'Tis a good place for a soldier to make a stand, Captain. With enough ammunition, three men could hold off a hundred Apaches from here."

It was sheltered from above by an overhang that reared a hundred feet or more to the mesa above. A small spring trickled out of a crevice at the back of an indentation in the side of the rock face. No horse could climb the steep slope up to this place, but there was ample sign that humans and small animals visited this place often, which was not surprising given the scarcity of water in this vast desert. Petroglyphs and smoke stains on the rock bespoke the fact that people had been camping here for millennia.

There was no firewood anywhere nearby, but the men had nothing to cook anyway and in this heat a man would not need a fire for warmth even during the coolest time of night.

Johnson said, "If they figure out we're here, we're trapped. There's no way out."

"Yes there is," said Macklin, pointing to one side of the shelter. "There's a trail that runs along there for about a hundred yards. It leads to a deep gap in the rock that goes all the way to the top. On the mesa above us and about two miles to the east, there are some abandoned mines."

"All over this desert there are abandoned mines," said Gately.

Macklin nodded. "But the nearest water to the mines I'm talking about is right there." He pointed to the seep at the back of the shelter. "At the top of the gap, the miners built a derrick with a winch where a man could be lowered down, along with some canvas water bags. He'd fill the bags and send them back up. Then they'd raise him up, and they'd carry the water back to the mines on mules or horses."

"How long ago did the miners leave?" asked Gately.

"They didn't leave," said Macklin. "Their bones are still up there. I helped bury them."

"Apaches?" asked Gately.

Macklin nodded.

"But the winch is still there?" said Johnson.

"It was there last time I was here."

"How long ago was that?"

"About two years."

"A lot can happen in two years. It'd be nice to know if it still is."

Macklin agreed. "Let's go see." Secretly he was not as confident as he tried to appear. When last he had viewed the derrick, it had been a rotted and rickety affair and the rope had been no better. The iron winch, however, though its gears were rusty and stiff, had still been functional.

With Macklin in the lead, they made their way along the trail and in a short time they reached the crevice. The thick rope was still hanging, and the iron hook, where a man would hang a water bag or place his foot for the ride to the top, was still attached.

"How's it anchored?" asked Gately, looking up at the derrick.

"They mounted it to the end of long poles laid flat on the ground and strapped side by side, then they piled big rocks on the other end of the poles. It would take a lot of weight to overbalance it."

Johnson shook his head and said, "Don't look very sturdy to me."

In the waning light of the evening, the three men stood gazing up at the old wooden derrick a hundred feet or so above them, and at the rotten-looking rope. Using them would be risky, they knew, but they would only do so if they had no other option.

Gately voiced what Macklin was thinking. "Between the two ways of dyin', Lads, I'll choose fallin' down the mountain. 'Twould be over in a matter of seconds. But death by Apache can be a long and unpleasant affair."

There was nothing more to be said. The men made their way back to the sheltering overhang.

"At least we won't die of thirst," said Gately when they got there, having taken a deep draft of sweet water from a freshly filled canteen. "A man can go a long while without eatin', as long as he's got water."

"I'll take the first watch," said Macklin, though his bones ached with fatigue.

"No, Captain," said Gately, "We've slept since you have. I'll take the first watch and Johnson the second. Get some rest."

Macklin didn't argue. Having no blanket now, he lay back in the powdery dirt and closed his eyes. He very much wished he could pull off his boots, but under the circumstances it would be foolish to do so. He was soon asleep.

Nothing happened on Gately's watch and when it was over he came in, yawning. He shook Johnson awake and said, "'Tis a quiet night out there. Maybe a little too quiet. Keep a close watch and stay awake."

"I've heard the Apaches don't usually attack at night."

"I've heard that too," said Sergeant Gately, "but I'm not sure the Apaches have heard it. Truth is, Lad, Apaches do whatever they want and it's not often what we expect them to do. You just keep your eyes and ears sharp, now, y'hear?"

Just outside the overhang, Johnson sat, straining his senses to detect any sign of Apaches. Not for the first time, he wished he had never volunteered for this mission. He was not like Macklin. He did not understand this desert. He could not identify every night sound. Macklin was a part of this place. He belonged here, and Johnson felt that he himself did not.

He had grown up in the forests of Pennsylvania, and now he thought of the sound of a breeze soughing through the pine trees—a sound that to him was the most peaceful and pleasant in the world. There were no pine trees in this desert; nothing but cacti and hostile brush with thorns that snatched and tore at a man's clothes and skin. There were no trees that grew much taller than a man sitting on a horse. He was a foreigner here.

The night wore on; the stars proceeded in their nightly march across the sky. Coyotes and night birds sent their calls into the warm breeze. Johnson dozed. Suddenly he lurched awake. What was that sound just now? Was it a lizard? A snake? An Apache? How could a man know?

The half-scream he made brought Macklin and Gately instantly out of their sleep and to their feet. Each man had slept with a pistol in his hand, and now Macklin heard Gately's gun roar and in its muzzle flash he saw the outline of an Apache, thrown backward by the impact of the slug.

There was a vague form just in front of him and he fired at it and heard the grunt that told him the bullet had struck home. To his left were sounds of a struggle and Gately's savage cursing. Macklin crossed the distance in the darkness, locating the Irishman by the sound of his cursing. By the light of the stars, he could dimly make out the form of the Apache Gately was grappling with. He put the muzzle of his pistol against the Apache's body and fired. "Back up against the rock, Gately," he shouted. "Stand beside me."

"Wait. Let me find my pistol."

"Find it. I'll cover you."

He heard the sounds of Gately groping on the floor of the shelter and then the Irishman breathed a hoarse, "All right."

Macklin felt Gately's presence next to him against the rock wall. "Johnson," murmured Gately. It was neither a question nor a statement. Johnson was dead. They both knew it.

"I'm going to light a match," said Macklin. "Be ready." He pulled a match from his pocket and, holding his colt at the ready, thumbed it alight. There were two dead Apaches on the floor of the shelter and one, badly wounded, who was crawling away. Gately dispatched him with a shot just before the match went out.

They found Johnson's body and afterward dragged the dead Apaches out of the shelter, rolling their bodies down the hill. Gately had torn a strip of cloth from Johnson's blue cavalry blouse and was wrapping it around his left hand.

Macklin said, "Let me see that. Keep watch while I do."

The hand had a deep knife gash all the way across the palm and was pouring blood. Using more of Johnson's blouse, Macklin made a pad of cloth and put it in the palm, wrapping it tightly with a cloth strip. "Now make a fist and the bleeding will stop," he said.

Because the shelter was not a cave, it was completely open except on the back side, and from within, a watchful man could see anything that approached from any direction. Neither Macklin nor Gately slept a wink the rest of that night, each man keeping careful watch on his half of the total world that was visible from the shelter. An hour or two before dawn, Macklin noted a change in the air. It was darker now and he knew it was because clouds were obscuring the stars.

Dawn came and it was a gloomy one, overcast by dark clouds; welcome clouds. It was time for the late summer rains, Macklin knew, and these clouds and the rains they heralded would be welcomed by all the inhabitants of the desert; animal, plant, and human alike.

It did not rain that day, however, though the clouds remained and significantly diffused the heat of the sun. Having no shovel for digging in the rocky earth, Macklin piled rocks on Johnson's body while Gately kept watch. Neither man made any further mention of Gately's knife wound, but Macklin could tell the man was in pain.

At dusk Macklin smelled smoke. A short time later he began seeing it—a lot of it.

"They're going to try to burn us out," he said to Gately. Quickly he began removing rocks from atop Johnson's body and, having uncovered one leg, he cut the leg off the trousers and then slit the cloth all the way down, creating a rectangle, which he then cut in half. Handing one of the halves to Gately, he said, "Make yourself a smoke mask."

Each man made his mask, cutting slits in it for eye holes, afterward saturating it with water and wrapping it around his face, tying it in back.

By now the desert below was completely aflame and the brush fire was spreading up the hill. The Apaches must have waited all day for a breeze that blew in the right direction, thought Macklin. That breeze carried the smoke directly up the hillside to where the two men sat waiting, each making frequent trips to the little seep at the back of the shelter to splash water on his smoke mask.

"Drink plenty of water," said Macklin, "and fill your canteen. When we leave here it will be on the run."

"The hawrses will be gone by now, Captain. You can be sure of that."

"Yes," agreed Macklin, "But they were too worn out to be much use to us anyway."

The entire desert in front of them and on both sides was burning now. The smoke and heat hit the rock face and were drawn upward. Macklin's eyes were burning and he closed them, knowing there was no risk of any Apache coming through the brush fire to attack them. He heard Gately coughing. They sat next to the little pool, constantly splashing water onto their makeshift smoke masks. The heat was almost unendurable.

Night came, and the only light was the light of the brush fire which was quickly burning itself out as it used up all the grass and brush in its path. Presently there was nothing left but glowing pinpoints everywhere—and the smoke.

Macklin said, "Sergeant, it's time to leave. Be ready for anything."

In the darkness and the choking smoke they made their way along the narrow trail, feeling their way with their hands on the rock face beside them. Macklin was in the lead and he found the gap by feel and touched the rope. "Wait for me here," he said. "There's a hook. When you feel me jerk on the rope, put one foot in the hook. You've only got one good hand, so hang on tight, understand?"

"Yes, Captain."

Macklin tested his weight on the rope a couple of times, praying it would hold. Then, using whatever footholds he could find by feel, he began pulling himself up, hand over hand, pushing with his legs.

The gap acted like a natural chimney and the smoke was concentrated here. Macklin began coughing and gasping. He started to feel lightheaded. "Not now," he moaned. This would be a very bad time to pass out. He stopped for a moment, wedging his back against one side of the gap, pushing with his feet against the other, trying to catch his breath but unable to do so because of the coughing.

Though he had tried to keep his eyes closed, tears were pouring out of them.

He forced calmness into his mind. He was working blindly. He had no idea how high he had climbed or how much farther he had to go, but there was a good man down there depending on him. He began climbing again.

Every few feet he had to stop to allow himself to cough and try and catch his breath. He concentrated all his energy on his grip, forcing his hands to grasp and pull. His feet found toe holds and pushed automatically without any conscious control. Even with his eyes closed he felt like he was spinning. Several times he felt his grip weaken and he slipped a short distance down the rope—how far, he had no way of knowing. Was he even moving upward, or was he slipping downward?

Suddenly his hand struck something. He groped around and identified it as a pulley. He had reached the bottom of the winch. The rest was easy. There was a good purchase for his feet and an iron bolt that stuck out from the derrick to grasp hold of. He pulled himself up and over the edge.

He crawled away from the derrick, away from the smoke, sucking in deep drafts of the clean air, coughing with each breath until he finally was able to breathe normally. His head cleared and he felt strength come back into his muscles. He pulled himself to his feet, ran back over to the winch, and gave a jerk on the rope.

The rope creaked and the derrick groaned as they took the big Irishman's weight, and Macklin prayed they would hold for just this one last trip, one last lift—this one last man.

With smoke blowing directly into his face once more, Macklin was again coughing and his eyes were streaming. It took all his strength to crank the winch and make the stiff, rusty gears turn. He could hear Gately's wheezing cough below him.

He knew the derrick was going to break before it broke. He heard the crackling of the wood just before it snapped and was able to seize the rope and shove the derrick and winch to one side with his shoulder. Now he leaned his body back, straining with all his might, pulling hand over hand, grateful each time he felt Gately take some of his own weight on his legs when he found a foothold. He could hear Gately's anguished groans and knew their cause: The

Irishman was having to grip the rope with his wounded hand, as well as with the good one.

There comes a time in every person's life when they are challenged beyond what they believe to be the limits of their endurance. What they do then is what separates those who fail from those who succeed. Somehow Macklin found strength where it seemed there was none remaining and presently Gately was pulling himself over the rim.

The two men lay side by side, beyond the smoke, coughing and pulling the clean air into their lungs. The broken part of the derrick lay on its side at the rim of the crevice and the, now useless, winch hung from it.

Hoarse from coughing Gately said, "My father always told me a man ought to have a new experience every day. The one I just had should cover six months' worth of days." He paused to cough a little and said, "I'll say this, Captain, I'm glad 'twas you on the top end of that rope and no other man."

"I'd like to return the compliment, Sergeant, but I'd have preferred a smaller man than yourself on the bottom end."

"I'll not be holdin' that against you, Captain. Not a bit."

After a brief rest, Macklin said, "I figure we have two hours at the most, before they figure out what we did and get on our trail. Let's make the most of those two hours."

"Aye," said Gately and after they had both taken a swig of water they started off.

With the thick blanket of dark clouds overhead and the pall of smoke that overhung the entire area, the night was nearly black and it was foolhardy for anyone to attempt to travel in the desert under the circumstances. Anyone, that was, except men who were being hunted by Apaches.

Macklin knew the way, knew the trail he wanted to follow, but he had some difficulty locating it in the darkness and even then, he wasn't completely sure he had found the right one. But it was a trail and as long as it led in the general direction he wanted to go, he would follow it. There was no other option.

A couple of hours before dawn a hard rain began pelting the desert. Gately exclaimed in a low voice, "Captain, the good Lard's lookin' out for us tonight. They'll never be able to find our trail now."

Macklin agreed with the Irishman, but he was taking no chances, and through the driving rain they kept up a fast pace. When dawn came they were miles away from where the Apaches had last seen them, and their trail had been obliterated by the rain.

They stopped for a brief rest, drank some water and refilled their canteens from one of the countless small streams that flowed now and would be nonexistent an hour after the rain stopped. Then, traveling faster, now that they could see the trail, glad they could move freely with no fear of raising dust, they pushed on.

The hard rain fell without let up until about an hour after dawn and then settled into a steady drizzle. The two men moved at a jogging run, putting ridges and bluffs and hills and canyons between them and the Apaches.

At midday they stopped to rest, and Macklin said, "Sergeant, let me see your hand."

"Ah, Captain, 'twill be as good as new in two or three days."

"Let me see it."

Macklin was unprepared for the sight he saw when he unwrapped the bandages. "It hurts, doesn't it?"

"A twinge now and then, Captain."

They washed it in clean rain water, then Macklin rinsed the bandage and wrapped it around the hand again.

Gately said, "We've missed our rendezvous with Captain Bitner."

"That'll mean a longer walk home for us," commented Macklin.

"When a man has come as close to dyin' as we did, he don't mind a bit of walkin'."

Macklin looked at the sky, which was starting to clear, and said, "We'll see how you feel about that when the sun comes out."

By midafternoon the clouds had cleared away and the sun had turned the desert into a humid hell. The sweat poured out of the men's bodies with no apparent cooling effect.

Fortunately, while they encountered no flowing streams, there were still pools of water everywhere, and they drank as much as they could, attempting to replace the moisture they were losing.

They spent the night at the base of a giant bluff, and though they took turns keeping watch, Macklin noticed that Gately slept little, if at all; his pain kept him awake. Macklin climbed to the top of the bluff, and spent the first half-hour after daylight lying flat on his stomach, screened by the brush that grew there, watching the countryside from the high vantage point.

He felt relatively certain the Apaches had no idea where he and Gately had gone. After the rain had started, he had made sure to not travel in a predictable direction, and, because of the rain, trying to find two men who didn't want to be found in this vast desert wasteland would be harder than finding a needle in ten haystacks. Nevertheless, he had learned to never underestimate Apache cunning and perseverance, so he watched.

Finally, having seen nothing that caused him concern, he said to Gately, "Let's go home."

"Home? Would you be takin' me to Ireland now?" asked the Irishman with a forced grin.

"If you start seeing anything around here that looks remotely like Ireland, look around for the Pearly Gates too, because they'll be nearby."

"Are ye sayin' we're lost Captain?" Without waiting for an answer, he said, "Two lost souls just sorchin' for salvation."

"You just hang on, Sergeant. I'm taking you to my home. We'll be there in time for mess."

Macklin took the most direct route he could over this rough terrain, and by noon they were on his land; shortly thereafter, they were standing by the burned-out remains of his house. Gately had been growing more pale and weak and feverish by the hour, and now he sat in the shade of one of the still-standing stone walls and drank deeply from his canteen, afterward leaning his head back and closing his eyes.

"Let me see the hand," said Macklin, and he removed the bandage. The smell that assailed his nostrils was as bad as the sight of the hand, and these, combined with the dark line that was moving up the wrist, told him everything he needed to know.

The Indians had completely ransacked the ranch buildings before burning them and there was not much left that was usable. But Apaches had no use for a shovel and Macklin found one, went into his house, cleared away some burnt debris, and began digging in the soft dirt near one of the corners.

Nearly three feet down he located what he knew was there, pulled it, out and carried it outside. It was a small, iron box that contained some money, a pistol, some ammunition, a few personal items that were meaningful to him, and a bottle of whiskey.

He uncorked the bottle and said to Gately, who still had his eyes closed, "Care for a swig of whiskey?"

The eyes came open and, seeing the bottle, Gately said, "Ah, Captain, the day an Irishman turns down a swig of whiskey, all the brim-fire lakes in hell will be froze solid." He drew deeply on the bottle, gave a thankful sigh, and offered the bottle back to Macklin, who shook his head. "Drink the whole thing, Sergeant. It'll help with the pain."

Gately's smile failed to erase the lines of pain on his face. He said, "A full bottle of whiskey in the middle of this unholy desert and me with permission to drink it all. In a minute I'll be hearin' the playin' of the harps."

While Gately was working on getting drunk, Macklin searched for certain items he would need. Most of his outbuildings had been burned, but his tool shed, though it had been ransacked, had been left intact—the Apaches apparently deeming it too small and insignificant to bother with—and he found within it most of the things he needed.

By this time the Irishman had fallen into a drunken sleep. Macklin spent a few minutes sharpening his axe with a file and he was ready.

He looked at Gately's hand agin. The ugly darkness was rapidly spreading upward, and he knew that what had to be done, had to be done immediately. He laid a half-burnt wood plank on the ground and strapped Gately's arm to it, afterward applying a tourniquet about four inches above the wrist.

Standing over Gately, he squared himself with the Irishman's bound arm and raised the axe above his head, holding it with both hands. He remained so for a few moments and then, hating the idea of what he was about to do, he murmured, "I'm sorry, Sergeant," and brought the axe down with all his strength.

When Dave Macklin and his two companions failed to appear at the rendezvous point, Captain Paul Bitner sent out several patrols in different directions to scout the area and see if they could see any sign of the three men. Late that afternoon, the sky to the east, many miles distant, filled with dark smoke. Corporal Rogers, standing nearby, said, "There's a brush fire over there, sir."

Bitner knew what it was, but he made no comment. He wondered if it had anything to do with the three missing men. Something told him it did.

The next day, the patrols returned empty-handed. Bitner waited until noon of the following day before ordering his men to mount up. He said, "Corporal, we'll ride to Contention and rest and water the horses there."

"Yes, sir." The corporal turned and gave the order, smiling secretly. Everyone on the post knew Bitner had a lady friend in Contention.

Bitner pulled up in front of the saloon, dismounted and turned the reins of his horse over to the corporal, saying, "Four hours."

The dimness inside the saloon gave him the momentary illusion of coolness, but the illusion was quickly dispelled by the hot, still air within. He asked for a beer and when it came, the bartender said, "Ain't cold, but it's wet."

Bitner drank deeply and looked in the mirror at his reflection. He hated himself for what he had done, and for the hundredth time he told himself he had done it for the right reasons. This was the army. Soldiers did dangerous things, and they sometimes died. Those three men had volunteered. He had not forced them to go. He drained the mug and ordered another beer.

Corporal Rogers rushed in and saluted. "Sir, Macklin and Sergeant Gately are over at the doctor's place."

Bitner made no attempt to hide his surprise. "Doctor's place? Someone hurt?"

"Gately lost a hand."

Bitner swore. "What about Johnson?"

"Apparently he's not with them, sir."

Swearing again, Bitner turned on his heel and strode out the door.

Having undergone surgery to remove a couple more inches of his left forearm, Gately was—thanks to the anesthetizing effects of laudanum—mercifully asleep.

Speaking to Macklin, Bitner said incredulously, "You chopped off his hand with an axe?"

"That's what I said at first," said Doctor Pope, who was standing beside the bed watching the sleeping Gately, "but he saved his life."

"Thank you for your services, Doctor," said Bitner. "The army will pay for any of Gately's expenses, and once you send word to me that he's ready to travel, I'll send an ambulance for him."

"Very well," agreed the doctor.

Outside, Bitner said to Macklin, 'What happened?"

Macklin gave him an abbreviated account of all that had happened since they had separated nearly a week ago.

"How did you get Gately to town without a horse?"

"I hoofed it to the road and caught some cowboys with a wagon, coming to town for supplies. We drove back to my place, loaded Gately in and drove directly here."

"What about the Apaches? Did you find them?"

"We found their camp. There's a pretty sizeable group of them. You'll need to get some men from Fort Rucker."

"Aren't there enough men at Lowell?"

"No. I'm telling you, Paul, unless you take enough men with you, you'll have another Little Big Horn on your hands."

"All right. I'll send a message to Rucker to send me as many men as they can spare. Let's plan on leaving at dawn two days from now."

Leave whenever you want, I'm not going with you."

"You're my scout. You're not going to lead me?"

"I'll draw you a good map, Paul. It's easy to find. I'll even help you plan the strategy, but I've done what you asked me to do. You won't need me for the rest of it."

"All right," said Bitner, "I was just hoping . . ." Whatever words he was about to say he brushed away with a wave of his hand. He simply said, "Make it a good map."

⌒‿‿⌒

Clara's patient was able to sit up now, and even make some feeble attempts at feeding himself. But still he did not speak, and still he only responded to questions with a nod or a shake of his head—and only to certain types of questions. To all other questions he made no attempt at all to respond.

He tired easily, and after being in an upright position for a just a few minutes, he would once again need to lie flat. Clara always knew when that moment came and removed the pillows that propped him up. She took the ruined suit of clothing he had been wearing when Howie and Bill had brought him into town and ordered a new set made, using the old clothes as a pattern. She did this secretly, knowing Doctor Pope would not approve.

There were times, when Clara would check on her patient, and find him covered with perspiration, his eyes squeezed shut, and his brow deeply furrowed. She was convinced, and the doctor agreed with her, that these were bad headaches. At these times Clara would sponge her patient's brow and place a cool, wet towel over his eyes and read to him in a soft voice. This always seemed to help and soon he would fall asleep, waking up hours later in no apparent pain.

His beard and hair had been allowed to grow unchecked, and now that his facial wounds had healed and he was able to be propped up for brief periods of time, Clara announced to the doctor that she was going to shave the patient.

"No. We'll bring the barber over, he can do it."

"The barber will charge; I'll do it for nothing."

"No, Clara, it's too . . . personal. It would be improper."

At this she laughed, and the doctor understood why: The care of a comatose patient involved things far more personal than a shave or a haircut.

The doctor clarified his position: "It's too wifely, Clara."

Her face flushed with embarrassment and anger and she left the room. But later that day the barber was brought in to shave the patient and cut his hair. The haircut came first and it was clearly all the patient could do to hold his head upright long enough for the barber to finish the job. Then the pillows were removed from behind his back and he was allowed to lie flat while the barber shaved him.

The transformation was dramatic, and the barber, not knowing whether to address Clara or her patient, spoke to the space between the two and said, "Not a bad lookin' face."

Marshal Johnny Belmont was still struggling to recover from his gunshot wound. He was pale and thin and lacking in energy. Shortly after returning from the desert, Macklin convinced him to consult Dr. Pope, and the doctor, after doing an examination, said, "You've got an infection in that lung. You'll have to stay here for a while."

Belmont turned and gave Macklin a look, and Macklin shook his head, "Not this time, Johnny."

But Belmont said, "Dave, it's only for a short while. I need you to do this for me. Anyway, what else you got to do?"

"Plenty," said Macklin. "I mean it, Johnny. Tell the town council to get someone else."

Word came that the army had successfully surrounded the Indians and, after a brief skirmish, forced them into submission. Macklin did not discuss with anyone his role in that victory, but Gately, during his brief stay at Doctor Pope's house, told and retold the story to anyone who would listen. Overnight, Dave Macklin, the acting marshal of Contention City, became the most popular man in town.

Word came that the army had successfully surrounded the Indians and, after a brief skirmish, forced them into submission. Macklin did not discuss with anyone his role in that victory, but Gately, during his brief stay at Doctor Pope's house, told and retold the story to anyone who would listen. Overnight, Dave Macklin, the acting marshal of Contention City, became the most popular man in town.

The alliance with Ben Lukert was turning out to be so profitable that Cliff Doyle was unwilling to do anything that may upset the arrangement. Accordingly, he tolerated criticism and blatant insults from Lukert that he would not have taken from any other living man. He was doing so at this moment and not liking it a bit. He was playing poker with Lukert and some of his men and had been winning steadily for the last hour.

"All I ever hear from you," Lukert was saying with a grin, "is how tough you Texans are. But Dave Macklin killed your brother and he's still walkin' around breathin' air."

"I'll take care of my business, Lukert, you take care of yours. Macklin's a dead man already. He just don't know it. You don't need to worry about him."

"I'm not worried at all, Doyle. If he ever raises any dust on my trail, I'll do the job myself. The man never lived that I was afraid of."

"And that same goes for me," said Doyle.

Lukert's smile said he doubted that statement.

Doyle resolved to put the issue of Macklin's longevity to rest. He greatly disliked the fact that Lukert thought him weak. He rose to his feet and said, "You and me, we get along pretty good, Lukert, but I want to get one thing straight. Macklin is for me to kill. I'll bide my time, I'll wait for my chance, and when it comes I'll kill him deader'n your great-grandma. Meanwhile, I expect you and your men to leave him alone. I want to get that as clear as rainwater between us."

Lukert's eyes narrowed. He didn't like being talked to in this manner. But finally he relaxed and smiled falsely. "All right, Doyle. Macklin means nothin' to me nohow. But he's the kind of man that can get in a man's way—if you know what I'm sayin'—and if he gets in my way—"

"You'll send for me," interrupted Doyle, "and I'll take care of him."

Up to this moment, Doyle had been uncharacteristically easygoing in his dealings with Lukert. And Lukert, as is typical of men of his ilk, had perceived this as timidity. But now he realized he had misjudged the man. He said, "Sure, Doyle. Like I said, Macklin don't mean a thing to me."

Doyle took his seat again and the poker game resumed, continuing for several more hours, during which time two of the five men sitting around the table dropped out, and one member of the gang, who had not been participating, came and sat down.

This was the way it always was at Lukert's hideout, Doyle observed to himself. There was almost always a poker game going on, and men would drop out and go eat something or get a few hours' sleep, only to return later.

There were two people in the group who always remained aloof from the rest of the gang. One of them was a young man who seldom spoke and was seldom spoken to; the other was a young woman who apparently did all the cooking and domestic chores for the entire gang. Doyle wondered about these two who did not seem to belong here, but he felt it would be unwise to ask too many questions.

Doyle had visited the outlaw hideout on a number of occasions, at times staying all night to play poker, but today was the first time he had ever seen Lukert speak to either of the two young people, and it was when they left the house together, saying they were going for a walk. Lukert said to them, "Don't go too far, you two," and he followed this statement with a mocking laugh. He then nodded to one of the men, who immediately got up and followed the pair.

Outside, the couple walked a short distance away to a pole corral where the young man turned his back to the rails, reclining against the top one. The woman faced him, and he saw the lines of exhaustion and worry in her face that only a few weeks ago had not been there.

Speaking in a low voice, she asked him, "Who is it this time?"

"Hart," said the young man, his voice equally low.

There was desperation in her tone when she spoke again. "What are we going to do, Phil? I can't take this anymore. The fear, the work, the way these men look at me, the filthy things they say to me. They're savages. It's making me old before my time."

He put his arms around her. "We've got to watch for our chance. It'll come. We just have to be ready."

"I'm afraid for you, Phil. He's just looking for an excuse to kill you. Please don't give him one."

"I don't know why he hasn't tried it already," said Phil.

"He can't do it without a good reason. The gang wouldn't stand for it. They would figure if he could do it to you, he could do it to any one of them. He would lose his control over them. He knows that."

Phil was silent. What she was saying was true. This gang was like a wolf pack. Phil's own brother had been its organizer and leader. Lukert had killed him and in so doing had become the dominant wolf in the pack. But he could lose that dominance if he made a single misstep.

Phil said to the woman, "I'm more afraid for you, Julia, than I am for myself."

"He won't do me any harm as long as you're alive. You have to be so careful. Things aren't like they were when Owen was here."

"I wish he—"

"He would have killed us, Phil." Julia said.

"Lukert reminds me of that almost every day; of how he saved our lives, saved us from my own brother."

"For what?" she said. "We both know why he saved me—and I'd rather be dead." She turned to him and took his hand between her two. She looked intently into his eyes and said, "I mean that, Phil. I'd rather be dead. When the time comes, I want you to remember I said that."

Clara's patient lay in the darkness, waiting for the pain in his head to subside so he could sleep. He was remembering things now. At first his thoughts had been vague and wispy things; disconnected, elusive. He had never been completely amnestic, had always known who he was, but his mental processes had been so disrupted that any attempt at concentrating on a particular thought had caused him to revert to unconsciousness.

Gradually, however, substance and clarity had returned. There were still blanks in his memory, like bare spots in a field of grass, but they did not worry him. He knew that in time they would fill in. The thing that did worry him was the partial paralysis of his left arm and his inability to form words. He could think words in his mind, but he simply could not speak them.

He was anxious to test his legs, but he knew it was not yet time for that—he was far too weak. Just sitting up was a chore. He had sensation in both legs and beneath the blankets that covered him he was able to move them. This gave him hope that he would walk again—in time.

CHAPTER 4

The mines were producing, the mills were running around the clock, the town was prospering and growing, and the Apaches were back on the reservation. The weather was cooling off, there had been plenty of rain recently, and the desert was green. Dave Macklin was acting as temporary town marshal of Contention City while Johnny Belmont recuperated.

Sally Pennington gave another party and everyone who came seemed to be happy. The food was almost as good as one would find in more civilized places. Sally and Nan sang several songs, which they had been practicing for weeks, and were wildly applauded by the group. There was a general atmosphere of goodwill and contentment.

Dave Macklin and Paul Bitner had both been invited, and Sally Pennington, who made all decisions regarding the seating arrangements, wisely seated the two men and Nan at places distant from each other. It would not do to stir up rivalry.

After the meal, Bitner, who had a much longer acquaintance with Nan than did Macklin, sought her out and invited her to take a walk with him in Sally's garden. As they left the room, they were observed by a good number of people, among them four women who were sitting clustered together, gossiping. One of the women had never been to one of Sally's occasions before and had not previously seen Paul Bitner. She remarked, "Well, he's certainly handsome."

Elona Chilter said, "Don't get any ideas, Dear, he's taken."

"They do look good together," commented another woman.

"They'll look good together at the altar too," said Elona, "because that's where they're headed." Elona often boasted that she knew more about the goings on in Contention than anyone else. And she loved to gossip. No confidence was safe with her, and what she did not know, she made up.

"Do you know that for a fact?" asked one of the women.

Smiling smugly, Elona nodded. "She told me herself."

In truth, no one had told Elona anything. She had been infatuated with Bitner since the first time she saw him and had taken advantage of every opportunity to fawn over him. It was quite apparent that Bitner was interested in Nan, and Elona could not imagine any woman rejecting such a man, so she felt safe in claiming to know for a fact something she was convinced could not possibly be otherwise.

Paul Bitner was not unaware of Mrs. Chilter's attitude toward him, but, while he was accustomed to that sort of thing from women and usually liked it, in this case he did not find it pleasing. He had once commented to a friend that being around Elona Chilter was like scraping his teeth across sandstone.

Sally's garden covered more than an acre, and, like her house, it had been designed with her guests in mind. Mature mesquite, manzanita, and paloverde trees had been transplanted here, along with as many different kinds of desert plants as could be found that were of the non-thorny variety. All through the garden there were poles from which hung lanterns for illumination, and many secluded spots where benches had been placed for private conversation. It was on one of these benches that Paul Bitner sat with Nan and said, "I've been wanting to speak to you, Nan."

Nan kept her expression neutral and her hands in her lap.

Bitner began, "First let me tell you that I expect to rise in the army. I've already been recommended for promotion for having put down the recent Apache uprising, and, looking forward, I anticipate having a very successful career. This posting out here in this Arizona wilderness is temporary, and once I've proven myself, which, frankly, I think I've already done, I intend to put in a request for transfer to a more desirable location. The money that I make now is not—"

Nan stopped him. "Paul," she said, "I'm honored, and I want you to know that I think very highly of you, but I'm not ready for this. Could we perhaps postpone this discussion?"

"Of course, Nan. I . . . I hope I haven't seemed too forward. It's just that in the army there is the tendency for haste. A man becomes accustomed—perhaps too accustomed—to doing things quickly, making quick decisions and then sticking by them. Those are things that are considered virtues in the military setting. But in matters like this, perhaps a man like myself would do well to learn some patience."

"I suppose patience is something we could all use a little more of," said Nan, keeping her comment as neutral as possible. "Shall we go back in? I believe it's time for dessert, and Sally has something special prepared for us."

Dave Macklin had watched as Nan and Bitner left the house, arm in arm, and he watched now as they returned. Nothing on either face told him anything, which was at once a relief and a disappointment.

He thought bitterly of the irony of the situation and wondered if it was his destiny that every woman he cared about should be snatched up by Paul Bitner, the man who had once been his best friend.

He knew, however, that he could not blame Bitner this time. The soldier could have no idea of Macklin's feelings for Nan. In fact, he was certain that Nan herself had no idea of those feelings. As for himself, Macklin had not known that Nan and Bitner even knew each other when his own feelings for Nan were conceived.

It occurred to him that this was either the wildest of coincidences or there was some kind of destiny he and Bitner had to work out together. He felt the old resentment for the man stirring within him, and he forced it back. He did not want to be churlish. Bitner had done nothing wrong in this case, and Macklin knew he had no justification for resentment. Moreover, he knew that to make a try for Nan would be a low and hypocritical thing to do. He had hated Bitner for years for having done the same thing to him.

There was yet another fact that he forced himself, with brutal honesty, to face: He could think of no reason why Nan should think twice about him. What did he have to offer a woman? Given a choice, Nan would surely choose Bitner. The soldier was a handsome man, full of charm and eloquence. He had his career ahead of him. He came from a wealthy family. When Macklin compared himself to Bitner he was convinced he was simply not in the game. He was a temporary town marshal living on a salary that was barely enough to support him alone.

He sat alone in a corner, realizing that even if he had tried he could not have stood in Bitner's way, and it occurred to him that Nan had probably already made her choice. If Bitner had not proposed marriage tonight out there in the garden, Macklin did not know the man as well as he thought, and he could think of no reason why Nan would have turned him down.

～～～

It was late afternoon when Cliff Doyle and three of his Double H riders rode into town and tied their ponies in front of The Bank Exchange Saloon. They went in and ordered drinks and when the bartender tried to collect his money, Doyle said, "We don't pay until we're finished."

The bartender was about to protest, but there was, about these Texans, something that stopped him.

The sun was going down when the four finally took their last drinks. Cliff Doyle picked up an empty whiskey bottle and hurled it into the mirror behind the bar. The bartender jumped out of the way as shards of glass, large and small, crashed downward.

There were two housemen in the saloon at the time, but before either of them could do anything, the Texans had their pistols out and had them covered. The Double H men may have been drinking, but they were far from drunk, and no one had any doubt of their ability or willingness to use their guns. The bartender noticed, however, that several patrons had slipped out the front door when Doyle had broken the mirror, and he was certain they would bring Dave Macklin, who was the acting marshal. But how Macklin would deal with these four wild cowboys he did not know.

As the minutes went by with no sign of Macklin, the bartender became increasingly worried. The four men were obviously waiting. He realized now that the entire incident had been prearranged. These Double H men were here to kill Dave Macklin.

Thirty minutes passed and then an hour, and still Macklin didn't come. Finally, Cliff Doyle gave a gloating laugh and said, "Let's go boys, we own this town."

When the bartender asked them to pay for the broken mirror and the liquor they had consumed, Doyle said, "Sure. Just send your brave marshal out to the Double H to collect it." They left the saloon, laughing.

It was dark outside, but the moon was bright. The Texans untied their horses and climbed into their saddles, but when they attempted to rein the horses around, the animals' movements were clumsy and awkward.

"My horse is hobbled," exclaimed one of the Texans in complete astonishment.

They were all hobbled.

From almost directly above them came a voice. "I'll kill the first one of you who goes for his gun."

The sight of Dave Macklin standing on the roof above them, outlined in the moonlight, pointing a shotgun at them, did away with any inclination any of them may have had to draw a weapon.

"Take your guns out with your left hands," ordered Macklin, "and drop 'em on the ground."

Now the two housemen came out of the saloon, both carrying sawed-off shotguns. Macklin said, "Cover them for me."

"With pleasure," said one of them.

Using a ladder he had leaned against the back wall of the Saloon, Macklin climbed down and came around front where he gathered up the reins of the horses. Speaking to the housemen, he said, "Stay with me while I lead these boys to the jail."

Cliff Doyle began shouting and cursing, completely losing control of his temper. He made desperate threats and swore such vile oaths that he began to draw a crowd.

At this time of evening, the saloons on either side of the street were filled with miners and millworkers, cowboys and teamsters, and all the other kinds of men and women who were to be found in such places in such a town. Many of them had been drawn out by the commotion, and they thronged the boardwalks on either side of the street.

Seeing Macklin lead three hobbled horses moving with their clumsly, comical gait, bearing these proud and quite unpopular Texas cowboys down the street in the bright moonlight, was cause for a great deal of mirth. By the time the Texans reached the jail, half the town was outside lining the streets, laughing at the spectacle.

Cliff Doyle was red-faced with fury. He cursed and made threats. He promised to kill Macklin and roast his guts over a fire. He kicked over the bunks in the cell and screamed and ranted for a good half hour before finally lapsing into a murderous silence.

And Macklin realized that one day he would have to kill this man—or be killed by him.

~⌒⌒~

Clara's patient could sit up now, and he could feed himself with his right hand. His left hand was practically useless; he could move it, but with minimal control and very little strength. His legs were weak and he would not trust them yet to support his weight, but they both seemed to work. Soon, he knew, he would be able to walk again. His memory was becoming much clearer as well. He did not remember what had happened to him, but he was beginning to remember things that he believed had to do with the event—had perhaps led up to it—and whenever he tried to focus on them, he began to feel a hot, killing rage building inside him, as though something that had been there before was returning; and his head began to ache unbearably.

~⌒⌒~

Gunfights were not uncommon occurrences in places like Contention City, and it was a generally accepted rule that as long as a fight was judged to be a fair one based on statements of witnesses, the law would not get involved.

Toby Elliott came out second-best in one of these gunfights. He and his two companions had robbed a bank in Colorado, and by the time they had shaken the posse that followed them, they were deep into Arizona territory and well on their way to Mexico.

They stopped at Contention for supplies and felt the urge to spend some of their stolen money on recreational activities. It did not occur to Toby that a man who possessed a third of what had recently been the contents of a bank vault in a prosperous town ought to be able to play cards without cheating. He had always cheated when he played cards and saw no reason to make an exception now.

One of the men whose money Toby took disagreed with this philosophy, and his subsequent accusations resulted in a gunfight. After it was over, Toby's two friends asked directions to the nearest doctor's office, and there they carried his limp body.

There was nothing Doctor Pope could do for Toby, except pronounce him dead and give his two friends directions to the undertaker's establishment. It seemed to the doctor that neither of Toby's friends seemed to be in any way upset about his demise. In fact, he could have sworn that just the reverse was true.

He was right. Toby's friends were not men of great erudition, but they both knew that half is more than a third—enough more, in this case, to assuage any grief they might have otherwise felt over the death of their comrade.

Walking past one of the rooms in Dr. Pope's clinic, one of the men happened to glance inside, and, seeing Clara's patient who was sitting up in bed, he said, "Owen! Owen is that you?"

He nudged his friend and said, "Hey look, it's Owen Meeker." They walked into the room. "Sorry to see you're ailin', Owen. Is there anything we can get you?"

A brief shake of the head was all the answer Clara's patient gave. The questioner was about to speak again, when someone pushed him aside and came into the room. Clara said, "I'm sorry, gentlemen, but he's been very ill and he's not ready for visitors yet."

After the two men were gone, Clara sat in a chair by the bed and said, "So it's Owen Meeker. Is that your name?"

There was a long pause, followed by a slight nod of the head and Clara felt betrayed by the reluctance of this man, for whom she had done so much, to share with her even so simple a thing as his name.

The next day, Clara came into the room to find Owen sitting on the side of the bed and she knew he wanted to leave. She also knew he wasn't ready. His legs were still too weak to support him and his coordination had not returned. But he wanted to go. And if he had been able to he would have.

And the thought left her feeling even more hurt and betrayed.

"Owen Meeker? Sure I've heard of him," said Macklin. "He's a gunman."

"Is he wanted for anything?" asked Doctor Pope, who had stopped Macklin on the street to question him about Meeker.

"I don't think so. I don't think anything's ever been proved against him. They say he's a mighty clever devil. It's claimed that he and his gang were pretty active around some of the Colorado mining towns up until recently. Why do you want to know, Doc?"

"He's the man Bill and Harve brought into town nearly dead; the one Clara's been taking care of at my place all this time."

"When did you find out who he is?"

"Yesterday."

Macklin rubbed his chin thoughtfully. "What are you going to do, Doc?"

"Not much we can do. He's still a patient, and I don't see him as any kind of threat. One of these days he'll be well enough to leave and he'll go."

"How about your bill? He must owe you a lot of money by now."

"He does, but knowing what I know I can't very well ask him for it."

"Why not?"

"What if he goes out and kills and robs some poor miner in order to pay me?"

Once again Macklin rubbed his chin. "Yeah, Doc I guess I can see your problem. Well if he gives you any trouble let me know."

"Thanks, Marshal, but I don't expect it." Pope started to turn away, then thought of something and said, "Marshal, would you mind keeping this under your hat? I don't want anyone knowing who we're taking care of at my place."

"Sure, Doc." Said Macklin. "I won't say a word to anyone."

The late summer rains came on schedule, and by fall the desert was well watered and green. The San Pedro was swiftly flowing and Mandy and Todd had to use the bridge to cross it rather than wading as they normally did. By mid-October, the weather was cooler. Summer was definitely over and the inhabitants of the desert looked forward now to half a year of mild weather.

Cliff Doyle's herd was growing, while those of surrounding ranches were shrinking. The Double H ranch and Ben Lukert's gang of outlaws were prospering. Doyle still had every intention of dealing with Macklin, but for the moment he was too busy rustling cattle for Lukert and his gang, to give Macklin much thought.

Now that it was safe to travel, Nan, accompanied by her mother, had gone back to Tucson to stay with her sister for a while, but she had promised her aunt Sally she would return within a month to help begin the preparations for Sally's Christmas party, an event that was looked forward to all year long by those who would be invited.

Macklin went out to his ranch, dug up his money box and removed all the cash. He had some debts to pay in Tucson that he had hoped to pay with the sale of his horses, and though his creditors, knowing his circumstances, were not pressing him, he felt it was time to pay up. After that, he would make one last effort to recover some of his horses, or at least get partial payment for them.

He took a stagecoach to Tucson from where he intended to go to San Carlos and look at the horses the soldiers had confiscated when they captured the Apache band. If he could find any with his brand on them he would attempt to get reimbursed for them by the army. He had, after all, been under contract to provide the army with horses when the very horses he was to sell them had been stolen.

He stayed a day in Tucson and settled his debts, afterward spending some time visiting friends. The following morning, he rented a horse and, joining up with the supply detail from Camp Grant, rode to the post, arriving just after tattoo on the second day. There, he was greeted by the camp commandant, Major Lewis, an old acquaintance.

"I suppose you're here to talk about horses," said Lewis. At Macklin's nod he said, "Good. We need 'em. How many you got?"

"None. That's why I'm here." Macklin then explained the purpose of his visit.

Lewis shook his head. "Sorry, Macklin. Any horses those Apaches had were confiscated by the army."

"Did the fact that some of them had my brand on them make any difference to the army, Major?"

"The army doesn't have to pay attention to brands. There's only one brand that matters to us, and that's the U. S."

"So, if a man steals an army horse," said Macklin, "he gets hanged."

"Correct," affirmed the major.

"But the army can steal my horses."

"Listen, Macklin. I'm charged with safeguarding an area of about twenty-five thousand square miles and protecting all the people and private property within it. And I've been given enough troopers to do an effective job of it in about twenty-five of those square miles. The whole area is infested with bandits and outlaws, road agents and Indians, and crooks of every species. There's no place on earth that has a bloodier history than this southwestern desert, and I don't see that changing anytime soon."

Macklin sat, impassively listening to the major's speech, all hope of getting anything out of the army already dead inside him.

The major continued, "And yet people keep coming here. Why they do is beyond me, but they do, and I'm supposed to protect them. I'm sorry about your horses, Macklin, but that's how it is."

Macklin ate in the mess hall that night and slept in the barracks, observing the banter and comaraderie between the soldiers, remembering when he had been one of them. In many ways, he missed those times. But not so much that he was tempted to return to that life.

He felt foolish for having come here. He should have known it would be this way. Lying on the bunk in the dark, listening to the chorus of snoring soldiers, he recognized that there was a lesson to be learned here and he made himself a promise never to forget it.

A man had his losses in life. It was a thing that was unavoidable. He needed to accept them and move forward, without looking back or worrying about who was to blame. Life was to blame, and it was the nature of life to bring successes and failures. Luck could smile at a man one day and coldly avert her face the next. Macklin decided then and there to waste no more time or effort—nor a minute more of sleep—on the matter of his lost horses. They were gone, and that was the end of it.

The next morning, he started back to Tucson. Two hours into the ride, he came upon a freight wagon with a broken wheel. He helped the freighters make the repair and then kept company with them for the rest of the trip, arriving in Tucson late Wednesday. The stage that went to Tombstone and nearby towns, including Contention City, left on Tuesdays and Fridays, so Macklin spent the next day killing time, loitering around town.

It was mid-morning. He was sitting on a plank bench outside the Palace Cigar Store, watching a Mexican parade, when he heard a familiar voice call his name. He turned to see Nan White approaching, walking arm in arm with a well-dressed, middle-aged man whose pot belly threatened to burst his vest.

Nan's smile was genuine, and Macklin found it a struggle to suppress the emotions that stirred inside him. He stood and removed his hat as she approached.

"I didn't expect to see you here," he said.

"Mother and I are visiting my sister."

"I'm just here—"

"On business," she interrupted. "And were you able to get your horses back?"

"No. How did you know about that?"

"We have a mutual friend. I was talking to Warren yesterday."

It surprised Macklin to learn that Nan had any interest at all in his doings. "Have you had an enjoyable visit?" he asked her.

"Yes, but I've been here nearly a month. It's time to get back to Contention. Aunt Sally needs some help." Then, as if suddenly remembering she was not alone, she said, "Oh, I've completely forgotten my manners." Turning to the man beside her, she said, "Jim Roush, this is Dave Macklin, a friend of mine from Contention City. Mr. Roush is a friend of the family."

Jim Roush was making little attempt to disguise the fact that he was annoyed by this distraction of Nan's attention. The two men shook hands, and Roush gave a mumbled, "Glad to meet you," and pulled on Nan's arm as if to draw her away.

But Nan stood firm, facing Macklin. She said, "Mr. Roush is taking me to the dance tonight at the Cosmopolitan. I'm sure you're planning on going."

Macklin was about to answer that he had no such plans, when he abruptly realized she was sending him a clear message with her eyes. He said, "Yes, it happens that I am."

"Well then," she said, "I'll guess we'll see you there."

He returned to his hotel room and lay on the bed for some time, thinking. Why had Nan greeted him in such a friendly manner on the street? Was it sincere, or was it simply because she needed his help in shedding Jim Roush, who seemed to be clinging to her like jumping cactus? Macklin could not keep himself from hoping there was more to it than that.

There was danger here, he knew. He felt his resolve weakening. He had promised himself he would not step into Paul Bitner's territory; not to do to Bitner what Bitner had once done to him. And yet it hardly seemed fair. Nan was a grown woman and should be permitted to make her own choice. But, by the same token, he grudgingly admitted to himself, the woman Bitner had stolen from him had also been an adult and free to choose.

It came down to a man's honor. And the fact that Bitner had had none did not justify dishonorable behavior on Macklin's part. Moreover, there was the unpleasant reality he had been forced to accept every time he had covered this same terrain in his mind: Given a choice between Bitner, the dashing soldier with the promising future, and himself, Macklin was convinced that any woman in her right mind would choose Bitner. She would be a fool not to.

This left him with an immediate dilemma. On the one hand, his sense of honor warned him to avoid Nan White, while on the other hand, he had promised her he would see her at the dance. What was the right thing to do?

He worried the problem around in his mind for some time before arriving at a solution. And it was one that brought him no sense of relief. In fact, as he reached for his hat and stepped out the door, he felt lonelier than he ever remembered feeling in his life.

The following morning at eight o'clock, the stagecoach left for Tombstone. Macklin was one of the first to board, and he sat there in depressed silence, paying little attention as other passengers boarded. The last to board was a woman, and she sat in the only remaining seat—directly across from him. He felt her eyes upon him and looked up. It was Nan. She was wearing a dove-grey traveling dress— a good choice, he thought, in view of the fact that it would be covered with dust by the time the trip ended.

"Hello, Miss White," he said, trying not to show the embarrassment he felt.

"Hello, Mr. Macklin," she said coolly.

Unable to think of anything else to say, he said, "How was the dance?" He immediately regretted bringing up the subject. He had broken his word to her and was embarrassed about it, knowing he could never explain his moral dilemma to her.

"It was . . ." She seemed unable to find an appropriate word to express her feelings about the dance. Finally, she said, "Fine. Your friend Mr. Williams is a very good dancer, very persistent as well. I suppose I need to thank you for sending him to . . . to watch out for me."

He felt his face flush. He looked down at his hat in his lap and turned it nervously. "Don't mention it," he mumbled. Changing the subject, he said, "Is your mother staying in Tucson?"

"Yes. My sister is expecting."

"Oh," he said.

Nan turned to look out the window. The conversation was over, and Macklin sat there feeling uncomfortable. It was going to be a long trip.

Roughly five hours after leaving Tucson, the stage stopped at the Cienega station, an old Butterfield stop, where the passengers were allowed to disembark, stretch their legs, and eat lunch while the horses were changed. From there it was straight on to Alamos, where they would have supper and spend the night, arising early to have breakfast and continue on the last leg of the journey.

It was between Cienega and Alamos, in the middle of the afternoon, that the road agents struck.

Coming around a blind bend in the trail, Charlie Davis, the driver, suddenly hauled on the reins as two men, each holding a shotgun pointed directly at him, stepped out from behind bushes. When the stage was stopped, two other men appeared, one on each side of the coach, and poked shotguns through the windows, stating in loud voices that anyone who made a move to pull a gun was dead. No one doubted them. All four men wore bandanas over the lower halves of their faces.

Stagecoach holdups had become such a problem in the area that a reward of five hundred dollars had been offered by one stage company to anyone who killed a holdup man, but this had not seemed to dissuade any but the most timorous and amateurish of holdup men. These bandits were clearly professionals.

The passengers were ordered out of the coach, and anything of value they carried on their persons was taken from them. Their baggage was removed from the boot and ransacked, money and valuables removed.

Lukert and his men had planned well. Each man knew his part. All four robbers carried shotguns and wore pistols in holsters. One man kept guard on the passengers, and another on Charlie Davis, while the other two confiscated everything of value they could find.

Macklin stood next to Nan during these proceedings, appearing, on the surface, calm, almost disinterested. The first thing that had been taken from him—followed by his watch and his money—was his gun. Not that he would have attempted to use it: to do so would have been extremely foolish and would have placed the other passengers in danger as well. A load of buckshot is not a thing to be scorned. There were four shotguns among this group of road agents, each with two barrels. It would have taken a man far less astute than Macklin to underestimate those odds. So he stood, seething with anger, but quiet and mute.

When the robbers had gotten what they wanted, one of them gave a whistle and a fifth man, also wearing a bandana, appeared from out of the brush, leading five horses. As his comrades were mounting their horses, the horse-holder's gaze fell on Macklin.

He turned and faced one of the mounted men, a big man wearing a dirty yellow shirt and, jerking a thumb over his shoulder, said, "That there's Macklin."

The one to whom he spoke turned his gaze on Macklin for a long moment and then growled, "Tie his hands."

Macklin's hands were tied in front of him with a leather thong while the man who had ordered this done withdrew leather gloves from his saddlebag and put them on. Macklin knew he was in for a beating.

The first punch was a solid right to the face, and it knocked Macklin back against the side of the coach. This was followed by a left, which knocked his head back against the window frame. Two more punches came in rapid succession, and Macklin found himself on his back on the ground. After giving him a vicious kick in the ribs the yellow-shirted man helped him to his feet and promptly knocked him down again.

Macklin rolled onto his stomach and pulled himself to his feet. The yellow-shirted man said, "You must want more." He swung his fist again, but believing Macklin to be beaten, he was careless. As the fist came toward him, Macklin's bound hands shot up and caught the man by the wrist. He jerked the outlaw toward him, lunging forward at the same time, head-butting the man on the nose. Macklin heard the crunch of cartilage and bone, felt it through his skull. Blood poured out of the outlaw's nose, immediately soaking the bandana he wore on his face.

Bellowing in pain and rage, the yellow-shirted man swung both fists, landing two solid blows that knocked Macklin on his back again. Raising a booted foot, he brought it down on Macklin's head, and Macklin lost all sensibility. The outlaw pulled his pistol and cocked it.

Nan screamed and threw herself on top of Macklin. "No," she said, "Don't do it."

Breathing hard from rage, the yellow-shirted man pointed his pistol at her and said, "Are you willin' to trade your life for his?"

"Yes," she said unhesitatingly.

He held the pistol steady, pointed directly at her head. Now, Charlie Davis, sitting up on his seat, spoke in an anguished voice. "Don't do it man, she's a woman."

The yellow-shirted man turned his pistol on Davis and said, "Then you'll have to give your life for hers. You ready for that?"

The driver was left with no options and everyone knew it. He nodded.

There was a long, tense moment while the yellow-shirted man held his pistol steady, aimed at the driver. Then, he lowered it, holstered it, and turned away, walking toward his horse. Blood still ran from his nose, covering the front of his yellow shirt.

Riding away, Ben Lukert was secretly glad the girl had done what she did. He was glad he had been stopped from killing Macklin, and he had never really intended to kill the girl or the driver. He had merely been saving face.

Lukert was a cautious outlaw. This was another thing he had learned from Owen Meeker. The robbing of a stagecoach was not a crime that elicited a major public outcry and brought posses and hordes of lawmen out to scour the desert for the malefactors, as would the cold-blooded murder of a passenger.

The events that had forced Meeker's gang to flee from Colorado had been precipitated by a killing, and they were still fresh in Lukert's mind. He wanted no repetition of those events here. Not that he had anything against murder, but he preferred to do it in secrecy and safety, not in front of a stagecoach full of people.

"Well, it's ruined. We'll never get the blood stains out of this dress."

"I don't care," said Nan. "It's just an old dress I wore for traveling." Freshly bathed, her dark hair still wet from the washing, she sat glumly in her nightdress and blue wrapper in her upstairs bedroom at Sally's house. Not understanding her niece's depression, Sally said cheerfully, "We'll have to invite Mr. Macklin over for dinner.

Nan shook her head.

Sally said, "But surely . . ."

"Oh, Aunt Sally, I feel like such a fool. I thought only men did these things."

Sally sat down and patted her niece on the knee. "What things, Dear?"

"Mr. Macklin has made it very clear that he has no interest whatsoever in me."

Sally leaned back. "I wouldn't be so—"

Nan interrupted, "I encountered him on the street in Tucson. I was with that horrid Mr. Roush who hounded me the entire time I was there. He had invited me to a dance, and I couldn't think of a good reason to say no, though I dreaded it. When we met Mr. Macklin, I invited him to the dance. I didn't think about how forward I was being and how that must look to him. He tried to demur, but I pressured him and he finally agreed."

"Well, Dear, sometimes a girl has to be a little assertive with a man like Mr. Macklin. I'm sure he didn't think anything of it. I would imagine he felt quite complimented in fact."

"You would imagine that, would you Aunt Sally? Well I guess that was part of my problem too. I imagined the same thing. But I was quite wrong."

"How so?"

"Apparently Mr. Macklin understood that I was wanting to free myself from Mr. Roush, but he finds my company so undesirable that he had to send someone else to do the job."

There was a long silence, and finally Sally said, "Of course I have no way of knowing why Mr. Macklin did what he did, but I can tell you this, Honey, there's not a man on earth who could possibly find your company undesirable."

After her niece had gone to bed, Sally remained in her sitting room as was her habit. But tonight she did not read. She put out the lights and sat in long contemplation. She loved her niece. Sally was the mother of three sons. To her, Nan was the daughter she had never had.

Sally Pennington was an observer of life and of human beings. She had a rare gift for understanding human nature and was rarely wrong in her judgements of people. And once a person was on her bad side, it was a long and difficult journey back. However, she was kind and fair in her judgements, preferring to like people when she could. And so, she was willing to overlook a great many flaws.

But the one sin for which there was no forgiveness in the heart of Sally Pennington was that of hurting someone she loved, especially if that someone was Nan or Milton. And Dave Macklin had done so. Sally did not understand this, and it was upon this enigma that she focused all her thoughts tonight as she sat alone in the dark.

She had liked Dave Macklin from the first time she had met him and had classified him loosely—as she did all people she met—into a particular category. She saw him as a man who possessed that particular sense of personal honor that she believed to be crucially important in an individual. Macklin was one of those rare men who, through something about them that was quite indefinable, was able, without trying, to gain the respect of other men almost immediately.

He was, she could tell, largely unaware of these things about himself, and Sally liked that about him too. He was a quiet man, never boastful.

She remembered how he had conducted himself in the gunfight that had taken place in her front room that awful night when Frank Doyle and his men had come in and interrupted her party. Macklin had calmly walked over and stood beside his friend, changing the odds from one against three to two against three. And Sally knew he would have done the same if the odds had been two against one hundred. He was that kind of man.

Sally was convinced Macklin was interested in Nan. She had observed him on a number of occasions as he had surreptitiously watched the girl. She had not yet plumbed the depth of his feelings, but she had no doubt he had them. Why, then, did he keep himself so aloof?

While Sally Pennington was pondering the enigma of Dave Macklin, her niece was lying in the darkness of her room doing the same. Nan was not an egotistical girl, but she would have had to be deaf and blind not to be aware of the fact that men found her attractive. And so, in one regard, she had, through no fault of her own, gained a certain amount of experience with men—chiefly in fending off the more aggressive ones and kindly deflecting the shy ones.

But she had never had a serious romance. There was, therefore, much about men that she did not understand. And she admitted to herself now, that she certainly did not understand Dave Macklin.

Elsewhere in the darkness, Dave Macklin lay, aching from his injuries and glad to be alive. When Nan had committed her bold act and saved his life, Macklin had not been conscious, but later at the Three Cottonwoods station, fellow passengers had recounted the event to him. Afterward, when he had attempted to thank her, Nan had been polite but reserved, something a man with a greater comprehension of the female psyche might have understood. But Dave Macklin was not that man.

Of one thing he was certain, however: The man who got Nan White for a wife—and he was pretty sure that man would be his old rival, Paul Bitner—would be a very lucky man.

And the thought set up an aching inside him that had nothing to do with the beating he had received.

⌒◡◡◠

Owen Meeker was beginning to regain his sense of balance, and when he had someone to lean on—and this was almost always Clara—he could take a few halting steps. His left leg, like his left arm, did not work as well as the right, but he was able, with effort, to slide it on the floor as he pulled himself along with the other leg. He was perfectly capable of feeding and shaving himself now, and Clara had turned those chores over to him.

But, though Meeker was becoming increasingly independent, communication with him had not improved. Dr. Pope said to Clara one day, "He's holding back. I'm convinced he can communicate far better than he's letting on."

"He can't talk," said Clara.

"I don't question that," said the doctor, "but he could use some form of hand signals. He doesn't want to communicate with us. I don't think he wants to answer questions."

Though outwardly Clara disagreed with the doctor, she was, in reality, in agreement. Meeker simply did not want to answer questions. And, why would he? she thought. He was an outlaw, a killer. Men like that had good reasons for not wanting to answer questions.

No longer did Clara sit by his bedside and read to him for long hours or speak to him cheering and encouraging thoughts. No longer did she wear a smile when she came into the room. The revelation of who he was had changed all that.

Clara knew she had no right to feel betrayed by him; he had not lied to her, nor had he told her he was someone he was not—these had been fantasies she had created herself—but she could not help feeling betrayed. She could not stop feeling angry. And now she only did for him that which was required by professional obligation.

The change in Clara did not go unnoticed by Meeker, nor was it difficult for him to deduce its cause: She had learned who he was. Meeker accepted this as he had accepted so many other things in his life, but he was deeply saddened by it. Though he tried to convince himself it did not matter; for the second time in his life, something good had come to him, and for the second time, it had been taken from him.

⌒‿‿⌒

Bo Creech was awakened by the insistent heat of the sun bearing down on him like a weight as he lay in a trash-strewn lot behind the main street of town. It took him a few moments to ascertain where he was and to remember the events of the previous night. Not that the previous night had been different from any other night in recent memory. He had gotten drunk, made a spectacle of himself, been ejected from the Head Light Saloon; where he and his spectacles were well-known; and had apparently staggered around to this place, collapsed, and slept until now.

He sat up and looked down at his body and for a moment was disgusted with himself. His disgust brought a moment of reflection on his past and on the ruin of his life, and he forced these thoughts out of his mind as quickly as they had come. He was good at that; he had been doing it for years. If life had taught him anything, it was to never look back and never think ahead beyond the current day: What would he do this day? Where would he get the money with which to sustain life and the demon within him that had driven him to destroy everything of worth he had ever possessed?

In his younger days, Bo Creech had been a bear-like giant who could out-eat, out-fight, out-work, and out-drink any man around. Now he was a lean, gaunt, big-boned man, who ate less and worked less than any man around, and generally only fought with the housemen who threw him out of saloons where he had worn out his welcome. But, though Bo was a drunk, the housemen knew—and if they didn't, they quickly learned—that there was still plenty of power behind those big fists.

Bo spent the next two hours trying find someone who was willing to give him money with which to buy whiskey. Having no success, he reluctantly decided he would have to find some way to earn the money, as he often did, doing odd jobs around town. But on this day, it seemed no one was in need of his services.

By late afternoon, he was suffering. He went out behind the saloon and begin sorting through the trash there in the hope of finding a bottle with even a little whiskey left in it, and it was there that Mandy and Todd saw him as they passed on their way home with some money they had just made.

Bo was talking to himself, kneeling on the ground, crying in desperation, throwing empty bottles, pounding the ground in anguish and frustration.

Something about the sight aroused sympathy in Mandy, and she approached him and said, "What's wrong, Bo?"

Bo had not realized until now, that he was not alone. He looked up at her, wiped his eyes with a dirty sleeve, and said, "Nothin's wrong. Be on your way."

"Don't look like nothin' to me."

Bo raised his voice and waved an arm, "Go away. Mind your own business."

"You're a drunk, aren't you? Everybody says that."

Bo clenched his fists and looked at her, scowling. He opened his mouth to speak harsh words and then stopped himself, and to Mandy, he appeared to hover for a moment between opposing emotions. All at once, his spirit seemed to collapse within him and he began to sob.

He knelt there, leaning forward, resting his scarred knuckles on the ground, and for a long time he held this position and shed the bitter tears of a broken and ruined man. When he finally stopped crying, he remembered the two kids. He sat on his haunches, wiped his face, and looked around. He was alone.

He glanced down at the ground in front of him and saw, lying there, some coins, neatly stacked. He picked them up and counted them. It wasn't a lot of money, but it was enough for today. And Bo had taught himself to never think beyond today.

❧

One night in early December, Nan and Sally were in the music room singing while Nan played accompaniment. For the two women, the nightly concert was the high point of the day. Sally's servants, who were generally all present, felt same way.

And so did Mandy, who rarely missed a night, sitting in the darkness of Sally Pennington's garden, hidden in the foliage just beyond the rectangle of light that came through the music room window. Todd sometimes stayed awake and listened to the music, but usually it lulled him to sleep. Mandy was always disappointed when, on cold nights, the window was shut. On those nights, she could still hear the music, but not as clearly as when the window was open.

Tonight was a warm night, and the windows of the house had been open all day. After several songs, Sally said to the assembled staff, "Any requests?"

Without thinking, Mandy blurted out, "Lorena," surprising herself by how loud her voice sounded in the stillness. She clapped her hand over her mouth and waited.

Todd was awake. He said, "We're in trouble now."

She shushed him. "Maybe they didn't hear."

"Then why aren't they singing?"

Minutes passed, and they waited. Then there was a shadow, standing above them in the darkness. They looked up—way up—at the high face of Edward, the butler. "You're wanted in the house," he said. He followed as Mandy and Todd walked around to the back door and into the kitchen. From there, they did not know the way. Edward led them to the music room. Mandy did not know what kind of trouble they were in. She knew they had been trespassing, but she was not sure how serious a crime that was.

Everyone was waiting. All eyes were on the two children as they entered. Sally Pennington said, "So, I take it you are music lovers."

"Yes, ma'am," said Mandy, self-consciously smoothing the front of her dress.

Turning to one of the servants, Sally said, "Susanna, I think we could all use some milk and cookies."

Susanna immediately rose and left the room, and Sally nodded to Nan, saying, "Lets sing Lorena."

Smiling, Nan began to play.

It was time for Clara's patient to leave. She knew it, and she could tell Owen Meeker did too. His left leg and hand were functioning, though not as well as the right, and he was able to walk and take care of himself.

Clara's ability to communicate with him had still not improved. He responded only to questions he wished to respond to. He never made any attempt to speak, and if asked a question that required more than an affirmative or negative response, he merely gazed at the questioner in a manner that quickly made the situation uncomfortable. On the day before he left, Clara asked him if he wanted to leave.

He nodded.

"Do you feel you are ready?"

He nodded.

"Do you have some place to go?"

He hesitated, then nodded.

"Do you have any money?"

He did not respond.

"Will you be all right?"

He nodded.

"Do I need to worry about you?"

He shook his head.

"Where . . .?" Clara stopped herself. Sometimes she slipped and asked questions she knew in advance he could not—or would not—answer. She withdrew a small purse from her pocket and started to open it, but Doctor Pope, who had insisted on being present at this interview, put his hand on hers. He said, "Mr. Meeker, Clara wants to loan you some money. If she does, can you pay her Back?"

Meeker nodded.

"Will you pay her back?"

Meeker nodded again.

"Soon?"

Again Meeker nodded.

The doctor removed his hand from Clara's, and as he turned away, he said, "The best of luck to you, sir."

Clara gave Meeker the money. He accepted it and put it in his pocket, and then did something he had never done before. He took her hand and kissed it.

Earlier, Clara had asked him if he would be staying in Contention, and he had shaken his head. So she had written the stagecoach schedules for him on a sheet of paper. If he went to Tucson, or south to Bisbee, Clara reasoned, it would probably mean he was leaving the area; perhaps returning to someplace more civilized, where his own people could care for him and assist him in making some kind of life for himself.

But if Meeker took the stage to Tombstone, it would indicate a probable intent to return to his old life. Tombstone was a trouble place, a wild and violent town, and to a man whose intentions were honest—unless he was able to do heavy labor like that of a miner or teamster—the town offered few opportunities.

After Meeker left the house, Clara followed him, telling herself she had the right to know where he was going. He went directly to the stage office and could be seen buying passage on the stagecoach. But to where? From the stage office, he went to the nearest saloon and disappeared within.

Clara went to the stage office and said to the attendant, "That man who just left—the one with the scarred face—where is he going?"

"Why, to Tombstone, ma'am."

Stony-faced, Clara turned away. She went to the small room she rented at a boardinghouse and closed the door behind her. Two hours later, when she emerged, her eyes were red.

When the stage to Tombstone pulled into Contention City, the driver reined in his team in front of McDermott's Saloon, and, while the passengers were having lunch and the horses were being changed, he went in and had a beer. Back outside, the passengers, including some new ones who were traveling from Contention to Tombstone, had boarded the stage. One of them was sitting on the box. There was nothing unusual in this, and the driver liked having someone to talk to while he drove.

This time, however, he was disappointed. The well-dressed man with the scarred face sitting next to him refused to speak, and soon the driver abandoned all efforts at conversation and drove in offended silence.

Leaving behind Contention City and the San Pedro river, the stage passed into the desert on its final leg to Tombstone. At about the halfway point, the man sitting on the box touched the driver on the shoulder, indicating with a gesture that he wanted to get off. Suddenly the driver realized this man must be a mute, and he felt mildly ashamed for having taken offense at what he thought was the man's rude refusal to converse.

"Here?" asked the driver, looking around. There was nothing here but desert. No dwellings or structures of any kind. "You sure?"

The man nodded. The driver reined in the horses, and the passenger took some time climbing down and then stood by the side of the road, clearly waiting for the stage to depart.

When it was out of sight in its own dust, Meeker walked a short distance from the road and found a place to lie on the ground. He had forgotten how difficult it was to ride on the box of a rocking, swaying coach. He felt as though he had expended all his energy just staying upright. He looked forward with great anticipation to the bed in the hotel room he would rent when he got to Tombstone. But, for now, after he rested, he had something important to do.

As an outlaw, Owen Meeker had been very successful. The mining camps of Montana and Colorado had offered rich pickings, and he and his band of killers and thieves had glutted themselves on the fruits of other men's labors until someone in his gang had been careless, and Meeker's protective sixth sense had warned him it was time to move on. He had then brought his gang here to the Tombstone area, where, under his able leadership, they had continued to prosper.

Most outlaws, including those in the Meeker gang, lived from job to job or, more accurately put, from robbery to robbery, taking their share of the loot and riding to some wild town like Tombstone or Pick-Em-Up, waking up a few days later with a hangover and nothing in their pockets but lint.

Meeker, however, was not like most outlaws. Not that he didn't sometimes partake of the pleasures of the raw hangouts, but when he did, he did so frugally and cautiously, spending no more than he had previously allotted himself. Consequently, he had, over the years, accumulated a large sum of money. And he did not save it in banks. He was not a trusting man. He was too much of a thief to have complete faith that anyone would be honest in caring for someone else's money. Moreover, banks were susceptible to robbery—as Meeker well knew.

After resting for nearly an hour, he climbed a low hill and, slowly turning a complete circle, scanned the area. Satisfied no one was around, he began walking, taking a course directly out into the desert. He knew exactly where he was, having long since memorized all the landmarks in this area. He had come here many times in the past—though always on horseback—to deposit money in his 'bank account in the ground,' as he called it. This time, however, he was going to withdraw a very large sum—all of it, in fact.

Meeker was well aware that he was far from being the man he had been before his injuries had nearly killed him. And he knew he never again would be that man. He was able to walk only short distances before having to sit down and rest, and his leg muscles, weak from long disuse, quickly began cramping. The spot he was headed for was about two miles from the road, and they were long and painful miles for Meeker. By the time he reached his destination, he wasn't entirely confident in his ability to make it back to the road.

He had chosen this spot with great care a number of years before, one of its most attractive features being a high bluff at the end of a narrow box canyon which branched off from another box canyon. The bluff had a flat top from which a man could see for miles in every direction. Meeker didn't bother attempting to climb the bluff this time; he simply did not have the strength to do it.

He rested for over an hour, then retrieved a small spade from a hiding place somewhat distant from the actual stash. Using the spade as a cane, he climbed the long, sloping talus pile to his hiding place in a recessed area at the base of the bluff. He dug up the metal box which contained every remaining cent of his accumulated wealth, emptied its contents into a cloth sack that was also in the box, and stuffed the sack into his shirt. He didn't bother returning the box to the hole, smoothing the earth around it, or wiping away his tracks as he had always done in the past. He had no intention of ever coming back here.

Weak as he was, it took Meeker several hours to make it back to the road, and there he sat on a rock and waited, his body bent forward, his head hanging down, the picture of exhaustion.

The road between Contention City and Tombstone was well-traveled. All the ore from the mines in Tombstone was taken to the mills at Millville and Contention City. Therefore, in addition to stagecoaches, horsemen, and other varied forms of traffic; there was, on the road, a constant back-and-forth flow of high-sided ore wagons, with their teams of many mules, that transported the ore from Tombstone to the mills along the San Pedro for the price of three dollars and fifty cents per ton. It was on one of these wagons that Meeker rode the remainder of the way into Tombstone, where he immediately went to the Grand Hotel, rented a room, drank a large amount of water, and slept for twelve hours, waking up sore and stiff.

CHAPTER 5

Macklin began making preparations to leave the area. He had finally come to terms with the fact that Nan would never be his, and, that being the case, he wanted to be as far away from her as possible, in the hope that distance would help to erase some of the pain.

He went over to Sally Pennington's to say goodbye to her and Nan, not looking forward to the chore, but feeling it was necessary.

Sally asked him, "Where are you going to go?"

Macklin had dreaded the question. "I'm not sure, ma'am. I was thinking maybe to Oregon. I've heard there are opportunities up there."

"That's a very long way, Mr. Macklin."

Nan was sitting alone on the other side of the room. Macklin glanced at her, hoping to see something on her face that might tell him that the thought of never seeing him again was in some way distressing to her. But her expression was as neutral as his own.

Sally walked outside with him along the front path to the tie rail. This was a thing he had never seen her do. She said, "A man who goes a far distance from home is generally either going toward a great opportunity or getting away from something. You said you're not even sure where you're going, so it's clear you're not heading toward a known opportunity. It's none of my business, but you must be trying to leave something behind. It would be presumptuous of me to ask what it is, so I won't. But I hope you are certain you're doing the right thing, and I wish you all the luck in the world." She took his hand and held it between her two palms for a moment, then she turned away and walked back toward the house.

Macklin watched her go, and it was then that he saw Nan standing in the doorway looking at him. The neutral expression her face had worn when he was saying goodbye was gone, replaced by one he now tried vainly to decipher. He caught her gaze and raised his hand in farewell. She raised hers too, and thus they remained for a long moment. Finally, he swung into the saddle, reined his horse around, and rode down the street, feeling her eyes on his back, wishing—wishing very hard, that things could be different.

He tried to push away the pain he was feeling. He tried to think of other things. In his mind, he listed the friends he had in Contention, mentally checking off the names of those to whom he had already said goodbye, ultimately finding significance in the fact that he had saved Sally Pennington and Nan for last. Then he remembered one last chore he needed to take care of.

Lena Carlson was out in the front yard, her arms up to her elbows in a washtub. Macklin felt sorry for this girl who was burdened with the task of raising her younger siblings while at the same time being the housekeeper for their grandfather. Lena was barely nineteen years old, but her pretty face was beginning to show the strain of the harshness of her life.

In order to make extra money, she sometimes took in washing, and Macklin, instead of using the Chinese laundry in town, preferred to give her his business. And he always gave her more money than she charged him.

When Lena saw Macklin, her wet hands unconsciously went to her hair, touching it, smoothing it. He dismounted and walked toward her, receiving her best Sunday-morning smile. She turned and went inside, bringing out his clothes, neatly folded and tied in a bundle.

He paid her, and she said, "You should marry me, Dave, and save a lot of money on laundry." In some company, Lena was shy, but she had aways felt comfortable around Macklin. It was her way to joke with him about his solitary bachelor's life, and they usually exchanged quips and mild, good-natured jibes afterward.

But this time, Macklin smiled and said, "Lena, the man who gets you will be one of the luckiest men in Arizona."

She came over to him and touched him on the arm. "What is it, Dave? What's happened?"

He told her he was leaving.

She tried to keep the hurt from showing in her eyes. "I hate to lose such a good customer," she said with false cheerfulness. Then she added, "Will you write to me?"

"Sure I will," said Macklin

"Have a good . . . have a good life, Dave."

"You too, Lena." He started to turn away, but she stopped him, pulling him around. She came close, and, holding his face in her two hands, pulled it down to hers and kissed him long and wistfully. Afterward she looked into his eyes for a long, searching moment and then, without another word, turned and walked into the house.

Feeling completely miserable, Macklin rode over to the Bank Exchange Saloon and went inside, more for the company than for the drink. Before going in, he noticed at the hitching rail three horses bearing the Star brand. When he had ordered his beer, the bartender said, pointing, "Three punchers over there lookin' for you."

Macklin turned. Three men wearing range clothes were sitting at a table, watching him. He walked over and said, "Lookin' for me?"

"You Dave Macklin?" asked the youngest of the three, who looked to be about eighteen years of age.

Macklin nodded, and the young man said, "Take a seat, if you don't mind."

Macklin sat and took a sip of his beer. The young man said, "We're from Star Ranch." Extending his hand, he said, "My name's Tony Nolan. My pa is the owner of Star. He wants to talk to you."

"I know your pa. What does he want to talk to me about?"

"Can't tell you."

"You don't know?"

"I know, but he wants to tell you hisself."

Tony Nolan seemed likable enough, and Macklin knew his father. The old man had done him a favor once, years ago. If Eli Nolan wanted to talk to him, he would go and talk.

It was not a short distance to the Star Ranch headquarters. The four men left Contention City mid-afternoon, and it was well after dark when they arrived at Star headquarters. During the ride, Macklin became somewhat acquainted with Tony Nolan and the other two riders. His judgment was that Tony was a young man trying to act more grown up than he was, and the two punchers were good men but not very experienced at ranching; certainly not the kind of men who had helped Eli Nolan build his Star spread.

At Star, the four men dismounted stiffly, and Tony took Macklin's reins, saying, "Go inside. I'll take care of your horse."

Macklin had never been to Star headquarters, and he was impressed by the size of the place. It bore the appearance of prosperity and industriousness on the outside, and on the inside it wore the marks of a place well cared for. The room he found himself in was a man's room. If a woman had ever left her stamp here, it had long ago been erased.

A bed had been brought into the room, and in that bed sat Eli Nolan. Macklin was shocked by the old man's appearance. He had only seen Eli twice before, the last time being two or three years previously. At that time, Eli had been robust and vital, looking every bit the kind of man it had taken to build a ranch like Star in this wild country. The man who sat in the bed was shriveled and frail—clearly not long for this world. His voice, when he spoke, was weak, but stronger than one would have expected from someone so enfeebled by illness.

Old Eli held out his hand and said, "Macklin, thanks for comin'. I was afraid the boys wouldn't find you."

Macklin was on the verge of telling him the boys had almost not found him; that if they had gone to Contention one day later they would have missed him. Instead he said, "It's good to see you, Eli. It's been a while."

Eli waved him to a seat, picked up a bell, and rang it. The sound drew a man into the room. He was a short, wiry, older man, looking spry despite a pronounced limp. His hair, somewhat dulled by age, was still red enough that anyone who saw him would know he was a redhead.

Eli said to him, "Bring us some food, Pete, and plenty of hot coffee. This here is Dave Macklin, and he's just had a long ride."

Pete shuffled over and held out his hand, bestowing upon Macklin a penetrating look.

"Pleasure," said Macklin as he shook the man's calloused hand. There was no weakness in Pete's grip.

Pete nodded. "Me too." He left the room.

Macklin knew old Eli to be a man who liked to come to the point, and he did so now.

"It's like this, Macklin. I'm done. I've lived a good, long life, but it's been a hard one and I'm tired, and I'm going to die."

Macklin smiled. "You make it sound like it's your choice, Eli."

Eli chuckled. "Well it ain't. But it's all right." He grew solemn. "In the mornin', I want you to walk around behind the house. You'll find a little graveyard back there. In it you'll find the graves of my wife and two of my three sons. You met Tony—he's the youngest.

He's a good boy. Makes me proud every day of his life, but he's not ready to run Star. I don't even think he wants to. The boy likes books. Talks about goin' to school back east somewhere. It's all nonsense and he'll outgrow it, but he'll need some time."

"How about your foreman?"

"Well, that's a problem," said Eli, shooting a glance toward the kitchen door. He spoke in a low voice, clearly not wanting Pete to hear what he was about to say. "It's like this: Pete was my foreman for years and years. I s'pose you could say we built this place together. Horse fell on him and lamed him a few years back. But even if he had two good legs, it's a job for a younger man. Since I've been sick, Pete has been sort of takin' charge. He hired a new foreman, and I don't think he's the man for the job. Listen, Macklin. What I aim to do is make you foreman of Star Ranch. Every man on this spread will do whatever you tell him to do, or he'll find himself ridin' down the road. And that includes Tony. You'll run the whole shebang until Tony is twenty-three years old. By then I think he'll be ready. You'll turn the northern half of Star over to him, and the southern half will be yours, free and clear. It meets up with your little spread, so you can tack that onto your acreage."

Eli watched Macklin's face intently, waiting for a response or a reaction of some kind. When Macklin said nothing, the old man continued, "Macklin, Star covers over two hundred thousand acres. Your piece of that will be a little over a hundred thousand. If you want to grow it bigger, then do it, but a hundred thousand acres ought to be enough for any man."

He leaned forward, holding out his hand to Macklin. "So what do you say, Macklin?"

Macklin did not make a move to shake hands. "No," he said.

Old Eli leaned back and put his hand down. "So you're turnin' me down?"

Macklin nodded.

"Never thought I'd meet a man who'd turn down a hundred thousand acres and all the cattle on it."

"Well you have now," said Macklin.

"Why?"

"Because it's not fair. I've done nothing to earn this. You have men working for you, why not take one of them and make him foreman?"

Eli reached over for his coffee cup and took a long swallow. He said, "You know how it is, Macklin. Most men on a spread like this are just cowhands. They do their work, pick up their thirty a month, ride into town on Saturday night, and leave most of it there. They come back drunk Sunday afternoon and start the week with a hangover. Most of them wouldn't take the job if you asked them; couldn't handle it if they did. I only had two hands that were foreman material. The first one was smart. He turned me down when I offered it to him. The second one took it. That was a month and a half ago. Three weeks ago, we found him and another hand dead. They'd been killed by rustlers. Which brings us to the part I hadn't told you yet."

"Why didn't you?"

"I wanted to see what you'd do when you thought you were getting somethin' for nothin'. You turned me down on that, which tells me more than ever that you're my man."

"What's the offer?"

"The offer's the same. But if you hold this place together for the next few years, you'll earn your half of Star. Fact is, Macklin, if you hold Star together for the next three months, you'll earn it. There's a band of rustlers that's feedin' off Star, and they're feedin' good. They're smart, and they're ruthless. They've already killed three of my men. And all three of them was old hands that had been with Star for years. So far we haven't been able to catch the men that did it, and we haven't figured out a way to stop the rustlin'. My men are discouraged—several of them have already quit. It's got to where I don't have anyone I trust to run this outfit. Tony would do it if I made him, but he doesn't want to and I wouldn't let him if he did. He's just not ready."

"But why give a man half the ranch?" asked Macklin.

Eli smiled sadly and looked away for a long moment. Presently he said, "A man can want too much, Macklin. When I started buildin' Star, I would have taken every acre of land I could get my hands on and as many head of beef as I could buy or raise. If I could have, I would have taken the whole of Arizona Territory and renamed it Star Ranch. But when a man bites off too much, he spends the rest of his life chewin' it. And then at the end of it all, he looks back and realizes that it's the only thing he ever did. A man don't need that much to be happy, Macklin. That's a lesson I wish I'd learned sooner."

Macklin had watched the old man's face as he talked, and he thought could sense the sorrow of all the years and all the losses Eli had lived through in his life. He had accomplished something few men ever did, and yet now, at the end of his life, it was unsatisfying to him.

Eli continued, "My boy's all I got left; him and Pete, and Pete's nearly as old as I am. I don't want to condemn my son to spend the rest of his life chewin' what I bit off. I want him to have more of a life than that. More of a life than I had. But it's going to take a man like you to give it to him. That's why I sent for you, Macklin. But if you fail, everything I built will soon be gone and you'll never get it back."

Eli lay his head back on his pillow, as if the talking he had done had taken too much of his waning strength. Presently he raised his head and said, "So now you know. It's a selfish offer I'm makin' you, and if you still want to turn it down I'll understand. You can bunk here tonight and ride away tomorrow and no hard feelings."

"No," said Macklin.

Eli smiled in resignation and laid his head back again.

"No," repeated Macklin, "I won't be riding away. I'll help you if I can. As far as your offer goes, we'll talk about it when all this is over."

"That's good enough for me," said Eli. And they shook hands.

The next day, Macklin began making preparations for war. After a few long discussions with Eli, Pete, Tony, and a few of the men, it became clear to him that Eli—probably because of age and infirmity—had not waged an aggressive campaign against the rustlers. Macklin was determined to do so. In a discussion with Eli, he said, "We've got to wipe the rustlers off the map."

He explained to Eli that the running of the ranch would have to be a secondary consideration; even such activities as roundups and branding of cattle, important as they were, may have to be set aside until the rustling problem was ended for good.

Eli said, "You're going to be shorthanded. Better hire another man or two."

Macklin agreed, saying, I'll ride into Benson tomorrow and see what I can scare up."

Eli added, "Piece of advice, Macklin. I wouldn't worry too much about their cow punchin' experience."

Macklin knew what Eli was saying. Right now Star needed fighting men, not cowmen. But finding them turned out not to be as easy as Macklin had hoped. Benson was a small town, and Macklin went into the few establishments, spreading the word about what he was seeking. But late in the day, he left town alone.

Part way back to the ranch, he noticed dust behind him and found a high point where he could see what was coming. It turned out to be a single rider who hailed him by name as he approached. "Are you, Macklin?"

Macklin nodded.

"Name's Sterling," the man said. He was a young man, not yet twenty years old, by Macklin's estimate, and he wore a bushy black beard, which, Macklin thought, may be to make him appear older. The horse he rode looked to have been a good horse at one time, but that time was long gone. His saddle appeared to be of the same vintage as the horse. His war bag was tied on behind it. He said, "Heard you were lookin' for a puncher."

Looking pointedly at the pistol in the kid's holster, Macklin said, "You know how to use that shootin' iron?"

"I can use it just fine, Mr. Macklin."

"Right now I need men to help me wipe out of a band of rustlers. There'll be some shooting involved. You interested in that?"

"I ain't doin' anything else at the moment."

Macklin liked the looks of the kid and he needed men, so he said, "Forty and found. Ten of that's fightin' wages."

"Best offer I've had all day," said Sterling. "When's chuck?"

On the way back to the ranch, Mackin noticed some tracks. After studying them for a while, he said, "Somebody's gettin' careless."

When they got back to the ranch, Macklin said to Tony, "I think we just got lucky. Let's round up the crew."

Joey Peck and Lane Mason had spent two days rounding up cattle in a distant corner of Star's range and were now driving the small herd they had gathered to the place where they were to rendezvous with the rest of the Double H crew.

Joey and Lane were part of the Doyles' original crew of ruffians and had come with them when they had been run out of Texas, mostly because the list of charges against them was every bit as long as that against the Doyle brothers.

There was no warning. They suddenly found themselves surrounded by men riding toward them from all directions. Escape was impossible, and they were too greatly outnumbered to try and shoot their way out of this.

Joey turned to his partner and said, "I think we're dead men."

And within twenty minutes, the riders of Star Ranch had proved him right.

The following morning, the stagecoach from Tombstone to Benson passed a tree with two corpses sitting propped up against it. The nooses they had been hanged with were still around their necks. Above their heads was a board on which had been painted the message: These men were caught rustling on Star Ranch.

Star had declared war.

～～～

Contention was not a large town, and the Carlson place was not far from Sally Pennington's house. Nan and Sally decided they could use the exercise, so they walked instead of taking a carriage.

Lena Carlson stepped outside to throw a pan of water in the yard and saw the two women approaching. She set the pan down and waited for them, looking somewhat apprehensive.

Smiling, Sally said, "We're here about your brother and sister."

Lena brushed a lock of hair away from her face. "What have they done now?"

"Nothing bad," said Sally, "but they seem to have too much free time on their hands. That can lead to trouble."

Lena's posture suggested an attitude of defensiveness, and Nan realized they would accomplish nothing if the girl felt she was being criticized for the way she was bringing up her younger siblings. Nan felt great compassion for this girl, not even as old as herself, who carried so much weight on her slender shoulders. She said, "Lena, we're not here to criticize you. I've always been impressed by Mandy's and Todd's manners and the fact that their clothes are always clean and mended. You are having to be both mother and father to them, and you are so young. How long have you been raising them?"

Lena seemed to relax. She said, "Our father died when I was eight. Mother died four years ago."

Sally said, "You're doing a fine job of being a parent, but you can't possibly do all that and be a school teacher too. That's why we're here. We'd like to help get those two kids educated."

Lena slowly nodded. "I would like that. They need some education, and I . . ." She stopped, as if she had almost said too much. "I can't give it to them."

Mandy and Todd came out of the house, from where they had been watching to see if they were in trouble. They politely greeted Sally and Nan.

Nan said to Lena, "Mrs. Pennington has a large library. If you'll allow the kids to come over every day, we can help them catch up with other students their ages, and they could then start riding the wagon over to Tombstone to go to school."

"Of course. That would be fine. Thank you."

"Our other reason for coming," said Sally, "was to invite you to an oyster party we're giving."

Lena's face brightened. "Why yes, I would love to. Dave, I mean Mr. Macklin, told me about your parties. He said they were wonderful."

"Yes," said Sally, "he was our guest a number of times."

"Lena kissed him," said Todd in childish candor. "I saw it."

Lena reddened. She turned to him and said, "Shush. Go in the house, both of you." She turned back to face the two women, clearly embarrassed.

There was an awkward moment, which Sally ended by saying, "Here's your invitation." She pulled a piece of paper from her purse and extended it.

Lena self-consciously wiped her hand on her dress before accepting the invitation. "Thank you," she said.

Macklin continued his preparations for the war with the rustlers. He checked the personal weapons of the Star punchers and found some of them to be antiquated and worn-out. He sent some men to Tucson with a wagon to buy supplies that would be needed. Those supplies included several rifles and pistols and a large supply of ammunition for both.

He spent the next few days riding the range, acquainting himself with the terrain and asking countless questions. Most of the Star riders were cooperative and friendly, though a few seemed to resent his presence. One of these was Max Holder, the man who had recently been made foreman by Pete and who had lost that position to Macklin.

Holder refused to speak to Macklin unless he was asked a direct question, and then he replied with as few words as possible, going out of his way to avoid being helpful.

When the supplies came back from Tucson, Macklin assembled the men. Everyone who worked for Star was present, even the cook. Eli was there, and he wanted to stand, supported on one side by Pete and on the other by his son.

He spoke just a few words, "Men, you all know the troubles we've been havin'. I brought Dave Macklin in to help us end them troubles. You've all met him now. He's my new foreman. I trust him, and I want you to trust him. If he gives an order, it's the same as if I gave that order. If he asks a question, it's like I was askin' it. If he hires a man, he don't have to ask my permission; the man's hired. If he tells you you're fired, don't come to me about it; you're down the road."

Eli's voice had become weaker as he spoke, and now he waved a hand to encompass the group and said to Macklin, "They're your men. Do whatever you have to do."

Pete and Tony assisted Eli back to the house and got him into bed.

Macklin said to the men, "From here on, consider yourselves to be in a war. If any of you don't feel like that's what you signed on for, you're right, it isn't. You can collect your pay and leave today, and no hard feelings. Those of you who stay will get ten dollars a month extra pay. If you decide to stay, you're to consider yourselves as soldiers in a war, and I'm your general. You'll do as you're told.

Before you make your decision, understand that before this war is over some of you might be dead."

Two of the punchers chose not to stay and fight. They were told to collect their gear, and they were paid off.

When they were gone, Macklin said, "Every man is to have a rifle and a pistol. If you lack one of them, Star will provide you with one. Every rifle we use will be of the same caliber, and all the pistols will be of the same caliber. Rifles will be .44-40 Winchester. Pistols will be .44 Colt. If you have a rifle or pistol that's the wrong caliber leave them in the bunkhouse."

Macklin understood that these measures might be unnecessary, but he had a military background, and in circumstances like these, a man's military training came to the fore.

When the inspection process was completed and every man was armed to Macklin's satisfaction, he said, "Every man will carry in his saddlebags at least a hundred rifle rounds and a hundred pistol rounds. No man will go anywhere unarmed. You will keep a weapon beside your bunk. You'll go armed to the cook shack. You'll go armed to the privy. If this ranch headquarters is ever attacked, I won't have men running around looking for a weapon. No man will go anywhere away from ranch headquarters alone. Wherever you go it will be in parties of at least three men. And you'll go nowhere without taking with you enough water to keep you alive for at least three days. If any of you don't understand these orders, raise your hand now."

No one did.

Macklin's next move was to cache food and water at some of the distant parts of the ranch. Tony, who had grown up on the ranch, assisted him in finding places where there would be water at least most of the year, as well as places of resort that would be highly defensible. They were all places where a small number of men could hold off a much larger force. In these places, he cached extra ammunition as well. He drew a map showing these locations, and all Star riders were required to memorize the map.

These preparations were accomplished in a matter of a few days. Macklin was wasting no time. He knew that every passing day found fewer cattle on Star, and the thought of this gave him a sense of the frustration Eli Nolan had been enduring.

Watching this ranch he had built being whittled away, its underpinnings eroded, and lacking the ability to stop it; knowing that, old and sick as he was, by the time he died, there may be nothing left to bequeath to his son, his only surviving heir, must have been hard to endure.

Macklin had hunted Apaches, and he had fought Apaches. He had killed Apaches, but he had never hated them. He understood their thinking and their grievances. He understood their way of life. He understood why they fought. They had their own way of looking at things; they saw the white man as their enemy, so they fought against the white man.

It was different with these outlaws. They did what they did and lived the way they lived because they were evil. They were not redressing any wrongs or fighting to preserve a way of life. They were selfish and wicked and cared nothing about the harm they inflicted on others. The men who were destroying Star were not doing it for the purpose of destroying Star; they were doing it simply because every head of beef they stole was money in their own pockets. And to them, nothing else mattered.

As far as Dave Macklin was concerned, every one of them deserved to die, and the world would be a better place when they did.

～～～

On the day Star Ranch began its war against the outlaws, Macklin divided the crew into groups of three, sending them to different parts of the range to scout for tracks. He took Tony and Holder with him to do the same. He wanted to locate the rustlers' headquarters, if possible, by following their tracks to and from that location.

"We've tried this before," explained Tony, "but they're smart."

This was a vast and rugged area, and the job Macklin was attempting to do with a handful of men would, in order to be done properly, require hundreds of men. The term needle in a haystack came into Macklin's mind, and then he reminded himself that needles don't leave trails. But, he thought wryly, they don't shoot at you either.

As if to underscore this thought, the sound of distant gun shots came from the east. He turned to Tony, who knew the area much better than he. "Which group?"

"I'd say it was Tyler's."

"Let's go."

Macklin knew there was little chance of getting to the spot where the shooting had occurred in time to do anything more than find out what had happened. The groups of men were spread over a wide area, and each trio was pretty much alone in the event of any trouble. They had started out at ranch headquarters earlier that morning, heading off in different directions like spokes of a wheel and, like spokes of a wheel, the farther away the groups got from headquarters the farther away they were from each other as well. And so Macklin and Tony and Holder pushed their horses hard, with the admittedly unrealistic hope of arriving in time to help if help was needed.

Presently, after riding for some time across rugged terrain, they saw the dust of a rider off to the southeast. Whoever was making the dust saw theirs and rode toward them. When the rider came into view, Tony said, "It's Sterling."

Visibly upset, Sterling said, "It's Art and Dwayne. They're dead."

"How'd it happen?" demanded Macklin.

"I don't know. We got separated and—"

Macklin interrupted, "I told you to stay together."

"I know, but we found two different sets of tracks. I followed one set, and they followed another. I heard shots and came around and found them. I found some tracks and I followed them, but they went into a dry wash where there were a lot of other tracks. I couldn't follow them very far. Then I figured I'd better let you know what happened."

They rode to the spot where the killings had occurred. The bodies of the two men were lying on the ground where they had fallen. Their horses were grazing nearby.

Sterling pointed to a nearby bluff and said, "The killer shot from up there. You can see where he wiped out his tracks. The wash is just over there."

Sick at heart, Macklin said, "Let's load 'em on their ponies."
This accomplished he said, "Sterling, you and Holder take 'em back.
Tony and I will see if we can follow the trail."

But Holder said, "I'll ride alone."

Sterling reddened and said, "You got somethin' against me,
Holder?"

Holder started to say something, but Macklin headed him off,
saying, "It only takes one man to lead two horses, Sterling. Go on
back to the ranch. Holder, you stay with us."

After Sterling left, Holder said, shaking his head, "Awful
strange."

Macklin knew what the man was thinking, and it worried him.
Sterling was, of course, the obvious suspect in these deaths.

Holder was pensive for a moment, then he said to Macklin, "I
guess I'll go back to the ranch."

"No, you stay with us," said Macklin.

"Art and Dwayne were friends of mine. I'm goin' back to help
take care of them. If you don't like it, fire me."

Macklin knew this was the first test of his authority. He
sympathized with Holder's feelings for his dead friends, but his
military training would not permit him to allow this kind of blatant
insubordination. He said, "Bury your friends and then pick up your
pay."

"Suits me," said Holder.

Macklin and Tony rode to the wash Sterling had pointed out.
The killer had been smart in using the dry wash as a getaway trail.
This desert was crisscrossed everywhere by cattle trails, and this wash
was part of one of those trails. It was full of tracks, and the coarse
sand allowed for no distinct hoof prints; only vague depressions
which made it impossible to distinguish between the prints of a horse
and those of cattle, or between fresh prints and old ones.

For more reasons than one, Macklin had hoped to find proof
that Sterling was not the killer—he, Macklin, was, after all, the one
who had brought Sterling to the ranch.

Darkness overtook them before they got back to Star
headquarters, and when they rode in to the yard, someone said from
the doorway of the house, "Tony, come in here."

Macklin said, "Go on. I'll take care of the horses."

As he turned the animals into the corral, the hostler came out and said, "You'd better get to the house, Macklin. You got troubles."

Macklin notice that most of the riders were not in the bunkhouse but were congregated in the yard as though they had been having some kind of meeting. The air in the yard seemed charged with animosity. He went directly to the house and went in without knocking. Eli was lying in the bed, and Macklin instantly realized the old rancher was dead.

Tony was already in the room, and he and Pete were standing beside the bed, their heads bowed in grief. Tony turned to look at Macklin as he came in the room, and there was no friendliness in his eyes. He said, "Star lost four men today."

"Four?" asked Macklin.

"Four, countin' Pa."

"Who was the other one?"

"Nick Jason. Somebody ambushed him. Shot him in the back."

Macklin was aware of men entering the room behind him, and the feeling in the room was decidedly hostile. He looked at the faces around him and knew he was in trouble.

"Where's Sterling?" he asked.

It was Holder who spoke. "Your helper; your hired gun, never came back."

Macklin felt someone slip his gun out of the holster. He was completely surrounded. Tony walked over to him and said, "You wanted it all, didn't you Macklin? Couldn't settle for half."

Macklin remained silent, knowing there was nothing he could say to this group that would ring true.

Standing next to him, Holder said, "We're going to string you up, Macklin."

All around him, men were speaking in angry voices. These men had lost four of their friends in one day. They needed someone to blame, and they needed someone to punish.

Rough hands grasped his arms. Rough hands tied his hands behind his back. There was pushing and shoving. One man was trying to get to him in order to slug him but couldn't get past the others who were manhandling him out of the room. Macklin knew there was no way out of this.

"Wait," a voice shouted above the din. It was Pete. "Stop it," he said. He faced Tony. "Tony you got to take charge here. This is your

116

ranch now," He turned toward the men who were holding Macklin. "You ain't got enough evidence to hang the man yet. Lock him up tonight. He'll keep 'til tomorrow. Somethin' like this needs to be done coolheaded."

He turned to look at Tony, their eyes met for a few moments, and Tony gave a quick nod. "He's right. He'll keep overnight. Let's make sure of what we're doin'."

There were some grumbles of dissent, but Pete had been a strong authority figure on the ranch since long before any of these men had worked here, and all of Tony's life. Tony showed his respect for that former authority by saying, "We'll do what Pete says."

"Tie his hands around the tie rail and let him hang on it," said Holder.

"That'll make for a rough night," said one man.

"You're right," said Holder, "Let's give him a feather bed with a nice, warm blanket, and you can fluff up his pillow."

Macklin was made to put one hand above the tie rail and one below it, and then his hands were tied together very tightly. There would be no way to find a comfortable position, he knew, but he also knew that an uncomfortable night was the least of his worries.

It was late when the last of the Star hands finally went to bed. The events of the day had created an atmosphere around the ranch that was not conducive to sleep. Forced to alternate between different extremely uncomfortable positions, Macklin's muscles began cramping. There would be no sleep for him tonight.

When the last of the lights was put out and the ranch was finally slumbering, Pete came out and sat on a chair on the porch not far away from Macklin. He was smoking a pipe. Instead of the verbal abuse Macklin expected, Pete began talking in a low voice, saying things that, under the circumstances seemed quite irrelevant.

"I'm going to miss Old Eli. We rode together for near forty years. His life was not an easy one. Except for me and Tony, he lost everyone he ever cared about. The Apaches killed Bob, his oldest. Rupert got bit by a rattler. We tried to save him, tried to cut out the poison, but he got gangrene. Doc came out from Benson and took off his leg, but . . . it was too late. And, you know, I never heard Eli complain. Not even when Alice died. Oh, he grieved . . . he grieved, but he never complained."

Pete puffed his pipe in silence for a while. Presently he said, "I'm sure going to miss him, Macklin, I surely am. He was a good judge of a man, Eli was. No ranch ever had a better crew than Star, and that's because Eli knew who to hire and who not to. He'd shake a man's hand, look right in his eye, and ask a few questions. That was all he needed. I never knew him to misjudge a man. For forty years I trusted his judgement, and I don't reckon I'm going to stop doin' that now."

He stopped talking for a time, then he said, "Macklin, Eli picked you. He told me you was the man to save Star." He chuckled. "Now, you yourself will have to admit you got off to a pretty rough start here. Ain't often a crew decides to lynch their foreman." He spent a few moments chuckling to himself, seeming to find great humor in the fact that the Star crew had tried to hang Macklin.

After a while he said, "I don't care so much about myself. It's Tony I worry about. He's a good boy. He's a real good boy."

Macklin tried to shift his cramped muscles during a long silence, while Pete puffed on his pipe. Finally, Pete began speaking again in the same low voice, "Most men, bein' in the situation you're in right now, if somebody was to cut their ropes and provide them with a horse, why, they'd ride away from here and not stop until they was so far away their own shadow wouldn't know where to find them. So my question to you is, what would you do?"

Macklin said, "Most men in my situation would tell you anything you wanted to hear to get you to let them go, and then you'd never see them again."

"That's true," admitted Pete. "But Eli trusted you, and I'm willin' to do the same. Tony's just a kid. He can't run this war. This spread is all he's got. If he loses it, he'll have nothin' ahead but a life as a thirty-a-month cow puncher. Star's all I've got too. At my age, what do I have to look forward to if the ranch is gone? Macklin, I'm askin' you to do what you can to help stop them rustlers."

"How can I do that? Any Star hand will have orders to kill me on sight."

"That's true. I'll do what I can about that, but meantime, you'll have to ride a twisty trail. All I need is your word."

"All right, Pete, you've got it."

"Thanks, Macklin. You're square. There's one other thing. That kid, Sterling. I liked him. I don't think he's a murderer any more than you are. I'd hate for his blood to be on Star's hands. Why don't you find him and keep him from trouble?" Bein' as how you brought him here, I think we'll both sleep easier if you see that he don't end up gettin' hanged or shot."

"All right, Pete. I'll do what I can."

Pete said, "There's a horse out back of the house, saddled. I packed a few supplies for you too. Don't make any noise." He produced a knife and sawed through the rope that bound Macklin's hands.

Rubbing his abraded wrists, Macklin said, "You're taking a big chance, Pete."

Pete said, "Eli started out ranchin' in Kansas. I rode in one day, broke, hungry, lookin' for a job. He hired me on. Wasn't long before I was his foreman. Eli was a little fiddle-footed in his younger days. He got to lookin' around and sayin', 'There's too many people here,' and right after the war, he decided on Arizona. We just packed up, drove the herd out here, and that's where the real story begins. Macklin, I've fought Apaches for Star, I've fought outlaws for Star, I've fought land-grabbers for Star. What I'm sayin' is, this ain't the first time I've took a risk for Star."

Macklin rode directly to the spot where the two men had been killed on the previous day and followed the same wash the killer had followed, reasoning that if the killer had been able to escape that way, he could do it too.

Moreover, as soon as it was light enough for tracking, he wanted to make another attempt at finding the killer's trail. He followed the wash in the darkness to where it entered a shallow canyon. The canyon walls grew higher as the wash penetrated deeper and passed the entrances to numerous side canyons.

He came to a place where the canyon forked and decided it would be best not to go any farther until daylight, when he would be able to get his bearings. Backtracking a few hundred yards, he entered a small side canyon.

He found a satisfactory spot, untied the blanket roll Pete had tied to the saddle, and found rolled in it a carbine, a coffee pot, some matches, and a can of coffee. He spread the blanket on the ground and opened the saddlebags. Pete had packed a pistol and ammunition, two full canteens, some jerky, a few hard biscuits, and some dried fruit. It wasn't a lot, but it was enough. Macklin knew all the locations where he had cached food and water for the Star riders. Tomorrow he would get more supplies.

He built a small fire, made some coffee, and lay back on his blanket, chewing jerky. He yawned and realized that it had been nearly twenty-four hours since he had slept.

From the shadows beside the house, Max Holder watched as Macklin rode away on the horse Pete had provided. Holder walked around to the front porch, where Pete sat smoking his pipe. In a low voice, Holder said, "What do you think he'll do?"

"What would you do?" said Pete.

"I wouldn't look back 'til I was halfway to Texas."

"That's you. But you ain't Macklin. He'll keep his word."

"You like to make things complicated, Pete. I like 'em simple. You could've told me you didn't want that Sterling kid to get hurt."

"If you'd stuck to the plan, I wouldn't've had to. How many times—"

"All right, all right. I don't need no more of your bullyraggin'.

"Then next time, do as you're told . . . and leave that kid alone."

Neal Sterling moved as silently as possible along the wash bed. He was afoot, having left his horse some distance back. He had been following the smell of campfire, and now he saw the dim glow of the dying embers as he approached Macklin's camp. It was quite dark here in the canyon, and he tried vainly to make out Macklin's blanket-wrapped form somewhere on the ground.

Suddenly a voice came from nearby, off to his right, accompanied by the click of a revolver being cocked. "Don't move."

"It's all right, Macklin."

"Go lay some wood on the fire. Try anything and I'll shoot you."

Sterling did as he was told, and soon the area was illuminated by the fire. Now, Macklin said, "Put your pistol on the ground and then move over to that rock and sit on it."

Sterling complied, and Macklin moved into the ring of light. He picked up Sterling's pistol, shoved it in his waistband, and said, "Take off your boots and throw them away from you."

Sterling did so.

"Take off your shirt."

Sterling took off his shirt.

"Toss it over where your boots are."

Sterling tossed the shirt.

Macklin said, "Take off your pants."

Now, Sterling stood there in his long, red underwear. Macklin said, "Turn around."

Sterling turned a circle and said, "Satisfied?"

"I just don't want to get back-shot like the last two men who trusted you."

"I didn't kill 'em, Macklin."

"And I supposed you're going to tell me you didn't come here to kill me."

"I didn't, and I can prove it."

"That would be interesting," said Macklin.

"Check the cylinder of my pistol."

Macklin checked it and then looked up and said, "It's empty."

"Check my boots, check my pants pockets, check my shirt—you won't find any bullets, no knife, no other weapons."

Macklin did the checking, then holstered his pistol and said, "Why?"

"You have a reputation, Macklin. You can track Apaches. I figure a man who can do that would be a hard man to sneak up on."

"Then why did you bring a pistol at all?"

"Just in case I needed to run a bluff. Listen, Macklin, I didn't kill those two men, and I don't know who did."

"Then why did you run away?"

"Why do you think?"

"You made it look like you and me were in cahoots. I almost got lynched for it."

"Maybe I'm tryin' to make up for that now."

"Maybe you are," said Macklin. He was thoughtful for a moment, remembering his promise to Pete to take care of this kid. He tossed Sterling's pistol back to him and said, "Better get some bullets in that thing. I think maybe you're going to need 'em."

The day after his arrival in Tombstone, Owen Meeker went to a gun shop and spent a good deal of time holding the different pistols there, cocking them, and examining their actions. Finally, having selected two, he used signs to show the gunsmith the modifications he wanted him to perform on them. The trigger pull was to be taken up, the barrels were to be shortened, and the pearl grips on one of them were to be replaced by wooden ones. When asked if he wanted the front sights replaced after the barrels were sawed off, Meeker shook his head.

After Meeker was gone, the gunsmith shook his own head and muttered, "Another would-be gun slinger. Won't last long in this town."

Several days later, when Meeker had picked up and paid for the pistols, along with a holster and shell belt and a long-bladed knife, he went back to his hotel room, where he remained most of the time during the following week. Meeker was a tall man, but he was not particularly large-boned, and he had small, almost feminine hands. From the very first, he was dissatisfied with the feel of the pistols' grips.

He procured a small wood rasp, some sandpaper, and a bottle of ink. He poured a small amount of ink into a water glass, diluted it with water, stirred it, and then dipped a piece of cloth into it, afterward smearing a light coating on the high points of his right hand, including the flat parts on the end of his fingers.

He chose the better of the two pistols to be his right-hand gun. He gripped the pistol with the stained hand and released it. When the ink had dried, he carefully studied the marks and then, using the rasp and sandpaper, he began working on the grips. With infinite care, he subtly contoured them, frequently holding the pistol, hefting it, pointing it, and dry firing.

Each morning for several days, when he was fresh and the memory of the feel of his gun was not strong, he would pull it from the holster, point and dry fire to see how it felt, invariably working on it some more, until finally, after several days of this, he was satisfied.

Now he went to work on the holster, oiling it inside and out, shoving the pistol down in it and pulling it out time after time after time. He determined the exact height to tie it on his thigh, the tightness of the belt. Everything had to be perfect.

He spent hours at a time practicing his handling of the pistol, growing accustomed to its feel, its every nuance. Making it so familiar that it might have been another part of his body.

After nearly two weeks of these preparations, Meeker gathered some empty cans from a back alley, rented a horse, and rode far out into the desert, where he began practicing with the loaded gun.

Day after day—bringing fresh cans—he rode to the same spot and spent hours practicing. One day, along with the empty cans, he brought six unopened cans of cooked tomatoes. After practicing on the empty cans, he set up the cans of tomatoes at different ranges all around him, even behind him. He checked the loads in the pistol, holstered it, pulled it, and began firing: right, left, turning to shoot behind him, then back to the front, pulling the trigger as fast as he could thumb the hammer back.

He stood there for a few moments, watching as the juice ran out of the cans—all six of them.

It looked a lot like blood.

CHAPTER 6

"Let's take the closed carriage today," said Sally Pennington to Nan. "It's been so long since it rained that the dust is six inches deep on the road."

"Where to, ma'am?" said Edward, who, in addition to being Sally's butler, was her driver.

"To Fairbank, Edward. To Mrs. Moore's house."

Nan did not enjoy Mrs. Moore' tea parties, but Sally insisted she attend. "I'll not allow you to make a hermit of yourself—nor a spinster, if I can help it."

Nan smiled dutifully but said nothing, and for a while the two women watched the countryside slip by as they traveled the few miles between Contention City and Fairbank.

Presently Sally said, "You're not very good company these days, Nan."

Nan turned to her and said, "I wasn't aware. Have I said something wrong?"

"You haven't said anything wrong. You haven't said much of anything at all."

"I'm sorry. It's just that I've been doing a lot of thinking."

"I would ask you what you are thinking so much about, but you would just lie to me."

"Lie?" said Nan, trying to put indignation she didn't feel into her inflection.

"All right, what have you been thinking about?"

Nan was pensive for a moment, then she laughed.

Sally said, "I can tell you haven't done much lying in your life. A good liar can come up with a story in an instant."

There was a pause, and then Sally said, "He'll be back, you know."

"From Oregon? I hardly think so. A man doesn't go that far away intending to come back anytime soon."

"The problem with you, Nan, is that you have no faith."

"Are we talking about religion now?"

"You have no faith in yourself."

Nan turned to face her aunt, her expression earnest, almost pleading. "Aunt Sally, what is wrong with me? I barely know him."

Sally took her hand and looked away. "I don't know how to explain these things, Dear. I just know that it happens. Sometimes, something whispers to a person, 'This is the one for you.' Maybe that's what you have to have faith in, Nan—that something, whatever it is."

The tea party was everything Nan had expected it to be: A lot of women older than herself gossiping about people, most of whom she didn't know.

The party was just getting started when Lena Carlson arrived. Nan and Sally had arranged for the girl to be invited, believing it would be good for her to begin socializing. Lena was wearing an old dress that was out of style, and she was obviously self-conscious. Nan heard Elona Chilter snigger, and Lena heard it too—she reddened.

Feeling immediately protective, Nan rose and called Lena over. She had been saving a chair for the girl in case she showed up, and now she said, "Sit here, Lena." When Lena was sitting, Nan leaned over and whispered to her, "Pay no attention to people who are jealous of your looks."

The party progressed, and after a time, the activities began. The first one was a reading. A short story was to be passed around, and each woman would take her turn reading a passage from it.

When the reading activity was announced, Nan heard Lena suck in her breath. She turned and saw the terror on the girl's face and surmised its cause. She doubted this girl had had much opportunity for schooling in her life. The book reached Nan first and she read a part. While she was reading, she reached for her cup of tea, fumbled, and spilled it squarely in Lena's lap. In the ensuing commotion, Nan smoothly passed the book to the woman sitting next to Lena and took the relieved girl outside, ostensibly to wipe off her dress.

Lena did not seem to be sure if the act had been accidental or intentional and when Nan apologized, she said, "It's just an old dress. Please don't worry about it."

"I'm afraid it's ruined. I will have to replace it."

"No, please, I can—"

"I insist. I will be very offended if you do not allow me to make amends for my clumsiness. You wouldn't offend me, would you?"

"Of course not, but I—"

"Then it's settled. No more talk."

Nan took her arm and said, "Let's take a turn around town and leave those women to do their gossiping."

They walked and conversed, and after a while Lena seemed to relax in Nan's affable presence.

The next day, Milton showed up at the Carlson residence with a wrapped package for Lena. Inside was a note from Nan and a beautiful blue dress; one of Nan's favorites.

~~~

Macklin and Sterling rose early and went to several of the places where Tony Nolan, under Macklin's direction, had cached supplies. They didn't have a pack animal, so they had to pack everything they could in Macklin's bedroll and their saddlebags. After they had cached the supplies in a new location, Sterling said, "What's your plan now, boss?"

"My plan has two parts," said Macklin. "The first part is to stay alive . . . and the second part I haven't come up with yet." Sterling burst into laughter. "You're an honest man, boss. Someday that might get you into trouble."

Sitting at the campfire a few hours later, eating canned beans, biscuits, and coffee, Macklin said, "The way I see it, you and I will have to fight like Apaches if we're going to help Star."

"Even if we do help Star, do you think Tony will honor Eli's promise to you?"

"Of course not. Not now—unless Pete talks him into it."

Sterling was silent for a time, and then he said, almost as if talking to himself, "Pete won't talk him into it."

"How do you know that?"

Sterling shook his head. "Just a feeling, that's all. But Boss, there's really no reason for either of us to hang around here tryin' to help people who want us dead."

"If you feel like you need to drift, kid, then go ahead and drift."

"No," said Sterling, "If you're stayin' I wouldn't want to leave and miss all the fun."

Macklin drained the last of the coffee from his cup, stood up and kicked dirt on the campfire. He climbed a small hill and spent considerable time with his field glasses, scanning the area.

When he came back down, he said to Sterling, "The way I see it, we've got to follow every trail on this range until we find the one the rustlers are using. Then we wait for them to use it again and follow them."

There was a pause as Sterling waited for more. And when it didn't come, he said, "And after that what's your plan?"

"Well, that plan has two parts. The first part is to stay alive."

"And the second part you haven't worked out yet," said Sterling with a grin.

"You're gettin' to be a real mind reader, Kid."

"One of my talents."

<hr />

Cliff Doyle had been an outlaw his entire life. He had been born into a family of outlaws, and one by one, his father and brothers had been either shot or hanged for their offenses—some of them during the commission thereof. And now, Cliff Doyle was the last of his line. He had been conditioned since childhood to hate the law, and along with it any figures of civil authority, and to despise anyone who believed in obeying the law. His was also a mind that had never recognized the illogic in hating those people who tried to protect what was rightfully theirs or to fight against him when he was robbing them. In short, he possessed the typical criminal mentality.

Star had caught two of his men rustling their cattle, and, in keeping with the law of the range, had hanged them. The fact that Doyle would have done the same to any man caught rustling Double H stock did not in any way attenuate the implacable hatred and the fierce anger he now felt toward the riders of Star Ranch.

He went outside and found a plank and cut it to length, afterward painting some lettering on it. He gave this sign board to his foreman, Floyd Colbert, telling him, "I want you to send a couple of men out. Tell them to find two Star riders, kill 'em, and set 'em by the road in the same spot where you found Lou and Greg."

Colbert grinned. "I'll go myself."

"No. You have other work to do. Lukert is whinin' that we ain't sendin' him enough beeves. You got to get to work on that."

Macklin and Sterling spent the next several days scouting trails and memorizing them as well as they could. There were quite a number of trails that bore the signs of recent use by cattle and horses, making the men wonder if the outlaws always used the same trail or if they tried to avoid being predictable by taking a different one each time. Or were there more than one group of rustlers?

How careful were the rustlers trying to be? Macklin wondered. This southern Arizona country was so rugged and vast that rustlers must feel almost immune to detection. There was grass here: There was graze for cattle, but it wasn't the lush, tall grass found in places with more rainfall and cooler temperatures; therefore, cattle on a desert ranch were spread over a much larger area than the same number of cattle would be in a wetter climate. This, combined with the ruggedness of the terrain, made a rancher's job a difficult one. And it made the job that Macklin and Sterling were attempting to do at this moment a seemingly impossible one.

After three days of riding, each man covering a different area, they met up again by prearrangement to discuss what they had learned. At the end of that discussion, Macklin summarized their information by saying, "Looks like the only way to catch the rustlers in the act is to get lucky; to happen to be on the trail they're using at the exact time they're using it."

The two men were tired of riding, and their horses were worn-out. The question now was what to do next. It was decided that the following day they would find a high point from which they could watch a large area with Macklin's field glasses and give their horses, and themselves, a rest.

They took turns being on lookout with the glasses, and it was late afternoon when Macklin heard a whistle from Sterling. Leaving the campsite where he had been resting in the shade of a rock,

Macklin went to where Sterling was lying belly-flat on the rim of the hill, and crept up beside him.

"What?" he queried.

"Southwest," said Sterling.

Macklin took the glasses and found what Sterling had been seeing: a tiny haze of dust.

"Could be anything," he said, "Could be wild horses."

"Could be the king of England," said Sterling. "It's been nice to rest, but I'm tired of layin' around."

"Yeah, me too. Let's go check it out. If it's nothing, we can camp there. I could do with a little change of scenery."

The Apache had been bitten by rattlesnakes before in his life and had survived, but this time he wasn't so sure he would. It had been a big snake, and it had bitten him twice. Now he was having visions and hearing voices. He thought they were the voices of his ancestors.

Narsi was the Apache's name. He was an outcast. Ostracized by members of his own tribe and hated and feared by whites because he was an Apache, he had, for a number of years, been living a solitary life. It was a life that suited him.

He was not a full-blooded Apache. He had been born in Mexico to a Yaqui woman. Narsi had remained among his mother's people until the age of twelve, when he was abducted by his Apache father and taken to live with his father's tribe in Arizona. He never accepted the Apaches as his people, and, when he was old enough, he returned to Mexico, only to find that his mother's Yaqui tribe had been massacred by Mexican soldiers.

Narsi lived alone for a number of years afterward, finally returning to his father's people in Arizona, where he was not warmly welcomed. Bitter, and angry at the world, he went to work as a scout for the army and in that capacity did things that made him even more unpopular with the Apaches.

He believed that his dead Apache ancestors hated him, and he thought it was possible that the rattlesnake that had bitten him was one of them. It had gone away very quickly, and he had not had a chance to kill it.

Maybe that was a good thing, he thought.

After being bitten, he had lain on the floor of his cave, for how long a time he did not know, until thirst drove him to get up and go to the place where there was water—a place known only to him and a few animals.

On the way back, he must have fallen. He must have gone into the sleep of sickness, and that was when the two white men had found him. When he awoke, he was in their camp. He woke to great pain. The pain of fire. Of something very hot being touched to his belly.

He saw the man above him, a white man. He saw his face as if looking through smoke or perhaps as if seeing him in a vision or a dream. The man laughed in an evil way and burned him again. And then Narsi knew this was no dream.

The white men—there were two of them—had found him and now would torture him. He understood this well—his people did it too. It was the way of things. He tried to clear his mind. He needed to take this the way an Apache would take it. He did not want to die screaming, as he had seen some white men die.

The white men kicked him, and he tried to guard himself from their kicks. It was then that he realized he was bound hand and foot. One of the men picked up a burning brand from the fire and brought it over, holding it close to Narsi's face. He told Narsi what he was going to do with it.

Narsi understood some English, and he understood what this man was saying. They were going to burn his eyes out. He would scream then, he knew. He would scream, and there would be no way he could keep from it.

From somewhere came a sharp-spoken command. The man above him spun around, dropping the brand next to Narsi's face. There was the loud popping sound of gun shots. The man fell across his body, quivering in death, and there were a few moments of silence. The brand was next to his face, and it was starting to burn his skin. He tried to move away from it.

And then someone was standing next to him, kicking the brand away, pulling the body of his dead enemy off him.

❧

Dave Macklin looked down at the two dead men on the ground and then at the Indian. He knew this man. They had been scouts together.

He cut Narsi's bonds and spoke a few words to him in Apache. He gave him some water, which the Indian sucked up greedily.

"He's got some pretty bad burns on him," Macklin said to Sterling. "They used a brandin' iron."

There was no response. Sterling was looking at the two dead men. He had killed one of them, and Macklin surmised by the kid's behavior now, that it was the first time he had killed a man.

They had stealthily approached what they thought to be a campfire in the fading light and observed the two men for a few minutes, wondering what they were doing. Then, changing his position, Macklin was able to see that the men had someone tied up, lying on the ground, and they were heating a branding iron over a fire.

Their intention was clear.

So engrossed were the two men in their torture that Macklin and Sterling easily sneaked up on them, and, when Macklin shouted at them to drop their guns, both men spun around, pulling their pistols. Macklin had shot one and Sterling the other.

Macklin poured some water over Narsi's burns, hoping to soothe the pain temporarily. He tried to help Narsi sit up, but the Apache was unable to do so.

Turning to Sterling, Macklin said, "Find a high point, and take a look around. We can spend the night here if it's safe."

Later, Sterling came back, looking pale and sick, saying, "Nobody around."

Macklin had already changed his mind. He had found the sign board strapped to the back of one of the saddles of the two dead men, and he now showed it to Sterling. It was a piece of one-inch thick plank about two feet long and ten inches wide. On it were painted the words, "These men were caught rustling Double H beef."

Sterling read the words and said, "A huntin' party?"

"That's right," said Macklin. "Somebody sent them over to hang some Star riders, and they probably planned to set them by the stage road with this sign hangin' above them. Just like we did to their men."

"But they ran across a sick, old Indian first and decided to have a little fun."

Macklin nodded. Narsi had told him about the snake bite. These men would never have even seen the Apache, much less captured him, had it not been for that. But, whoever had made the sign board had made a very foolish mistake. That person had as much as admitted that the two rustlers Star had hanged were from the Double H.

"So what's your plan?" asked Sterling.

"Well, it sure seems a shame to waste a good sign board."

"What about him?" Sterling said, indicating the Apache.

"Not much we can do for him, except make sure he has plenty of water."

He handed his canteen to Narsi and told him to drink. With trembling hands, the Apache did so. And when he handed the canteen back, Macklin told him to keep it.

He rolled out the bedroll of one of the dead men and found a place that would be in the shade tomorrow when the sun came out. He picked up the Apache and carried him over, placing him on the blanket. He brought the canteen and laid it beside the Apache and said, "There's plenty of water in it. We'll be back tomorrow."

Narsi nodded.

～ ～ ～

"Are they back yet?" asked Doyle of his foreman, Floyd Colbert.

"Not yet," replied Colbert.

"If they went over into Pick-Em-Up, carousin', then they're finished on Double H," said Doyle.

"They're probably just havin' a hard time findin' any Star riders to kill."

Doyle snorted his disbelief of this comment. "Ride into Benson," he ordered, "and nose around. If they did what they were told to do, the whole town'll be talkin' about it."

Late that afternoon, the foreman and the two men who had gone with him returned to Double H.

Doyle came out to meet them. "Well, did you find 'em?"

"Yeah we found 'em," said Colbert. "We found 'em on the stage road sittin' beneath this sign."

He showed Doyle the sign, and Doyle recognized it as the one he himself had made. The end had been broken off, removing the words "from Double H," making the sign read, "These men were caught rustling." Doyle's face hardened; his jaw muscles worked, cording like ropes. He uttered one word. "Star."

"I don't think so," said Colbert. "I'm thinkin' it was Macklin and the Sterling kid."

"Why do you think that?" said Doyle.

"Max left a letter for us in Benson. Accordin' to what it says, Old Eli's dead, and the Star crew run Macklin off, and now Sterling is with him."

He pulled a wrinkled envelope from inside his shirt and handed it to Doyle, who read it slowly and said, "I thought that kid was going to be on our side."

Colbert shrugged. "Maybe he still is."

Doyle cursed vehemently. "We've lost near half our crew in the past month, and Macklin's the one behind it."

They were in the main room of the small, tumble-down house the Double H called its headquarters. To the west of the house sat the bunkhouse and the cook shack. An assortment of other buildings, mostly sheds, all of them as run-down in appearance as the main house, were scattered around the area in what must have been someone's idea of an efficient arrangement.

The Doyle brothers had not purchased the Double H; they had stolen it from a cousin. When they and their crew of riffraff had been run out of Texas, they had left with a small herd of stolen cattle and picked up more on the way, arriving in Arizona with a moderate-sized herd, most of them with altered brands.

Having little choice, the cousin had reluctantly agreed to allow the Doyles and their men to stay for a few weeks and graze their herd on his range until they found their own spread. The few weeks turned to six months, which became a year, during which time nearly all the men in the cousin's employ had quit, either out of fear of the Doyles' crew of hard cases or simply because they did not choose to associate with such men. In the end, the elder Doyle, Frank, had quarreled with the cousin and killed him in a gunfight. And the ranch belonged to Frank and Cliff.

Frank and Cliff Doyle and their men had done nothing to improve the place; in fact, it had become more dilapidated during the time of their occupancy than it had been before their arrival. These were not industrious men. Like most criminals, they had chosen the path of crime because they were essentially lazy.

Doyle said to Floyd Colbert, "Send out some men to find Macklin and that kid. I want 'em dead, both of them. And I want Tony Nolan dead. Now that Eli's gone, with the three of them out of the way and Pete dead, the star crew will fall apart."

"Pete ain't dead," pointed out Colbert.

"Ain't he?" said Doyle, a malevolent glint in his eye. "Maybe he just ain't figured it out yet. Get a message to him. Tell him I want to meet with him at the same spot, three days from now, at noon."

When Macklin and Sterling returned to the place where they had left the Apache, they found him somewhat improved, lying on his back, with some sort of poultice made from plants and clay plastered on his burned stomach.

Macklin made some coffee and food and offered him some. The Apache refused the coffee, preferring water, but he ate a small amount of food and then fell asleep. His face was stoic, but there were lines of suffering that had not been there the previous day.

After they had eaten, Sterling asked, "What now?"

"We'll stay with him two or three days until he's well enough to go wherever he wants to."

"Stay here? What for?"

"Just about any white man would kill an Apache on sight," said Macklin. "He's not strong enough to defend himself or get away."

"He's just an Indian," said Sterling. "Let him take care of himself. If he dies, he dies."

"He's a friend of mine," snapped Macklin. "If you want to go somewhere, nobody's stoppin' you."

"Maybe I will," said Sterling sulkily. But he stayed around camp, maintaining a stubborn, sullen, silence until the next morning.

Macklin did what little he could for the Apache, but mostly the man took care of himself, struggling to his feet and staggering out into the desert, returning sometime afterward with materials he needed for his poultices.

He improved quite quickly, and each day his appetite grew and his strength increased. During this time, Macklin and Sterling made frequent forays, always in different directions, out into the desert, searching out new trails and learning everything they could about them.

One morning they awoke, and the Apache was gone. Neither of the two commented on this, but they continued with their riding and mapping and searching.

On the appointed day, as Doyle and his men rode toward the meeting place, Doyle's alert eye caught a flash of sunlight on something shiny.

"He's watchin' us with a glass," he commented.

When they reached the location, they reined in their horses and waited. Doyle fashioned a cigarette and casually puffed it, his eyes constantly moving, keenly alert. The men with him were uneasy, suspecting a trap. But Doyle did not suspect a trap. He thought he knew what Pete's purposes were, and a trap would not suit those purposes.

"He's comin'," said one of the men. Doyle saw Pete now, riding toward them. He noted the easy way the old man sat in the saddle, how he handled his horse. His accident had ruined him for walking, but he had spent his life in the saddle and had no difficulty at all in riding.

Pete reined in in front of Doyle and said, "Good to see you, Doyle."

Doyle nodded curtly.

Pete said, "Things has changed a bit on Star."

"They've changed a bit on Double H too. My crew has got considerable smaller. This thing ain't working like you promised, Pete. You been telling us that when Eli was dead, things would change."

"They will."

"How's that?"

"It's time for me to take over Star," declared Pete.

Doyle gazed at the old man for a few moments, and a wicked smile came onto his face. He said, "You going to kill Eli's boy, or do we do it?"

"Now, about that," said Pete, "Don't forget what we agreed on. I don't want Tony killed. There's other ways."

Doyle's smile remained, but he said nothing.

Pete said, "Doyle, you've done what we agreed on; now it's time for us to part ways."

"Part ways?" said Doyle. "Why, things has just started gettin' interesting."

Pete said, "Star can't afford to lose any more beef. You've done your part, and I've done mine. We agreed that when I said stop, you'd stop. Well, that time's come. You must've made a passel of money on this caper, but it's time to—"

Doyle spurred his horse over to where Pete sat on his mount, reached over, and hooked an elbow around the old man's neck, then spurred his horse away, dragging Pete out of the saddle, holding him so his boots were just a few inches off the ground.

Pete gagged and kicked, clawing at Doyle's thick arm with his fingers, trying to get loose, but Doyle kept his forearm clamped across Pete's neck until the wiry old man quit struggling, and then he held him a little while longer, finally spurring back over to Pete's horse, where he draped the limp body over the saddle. Reaching down, he took the bridle reins and said to his men, "Let's go."

"Why didn't you just shoot him, Boss?" asked Floyd Colbert, spurring up alongside Doyle.

"You got to be quiet whenever you can. Never know who a shot will draw."

Floyd didn't comment on this, but he had seen the pleasure on Doyle's face as Pete's life had drained out of him. Doyle had enjoyed killing the old man. As for Floyd, he did not condemn his boss for being a ghoul; he had enjoyed watching.

One morning, as Macklin and Sterling were eating their breakfast, Narsi walked into camp. Without speaking, he sat and waited while they cooked some more bacon and fed him. Then, he went out to where the horses of the two dead Double H riders were picketed and brought one back, leading him on a hackamore.

He said to Macklin in Apache, "Follow me," and, slipping onto the horse's bare back, he rode away. He led them to a deep wash with a sandy bottom and pointed to a spot that appeared to have been recently disturbed.

He knelt down and began digging with his hands until he had partially uncovered the torso and head of a man. The red hair of the corpse made identification instantaneous. Macklin heard Sterling, standing next to him, give a gasp.

"It can't be," the young man said, "It's . . . it can't be him."

Macklin looked at him, confused. As far as he knew, Sterling had barely known Pete.

Sterling turned away and walked to his horse and rode back to camp. Macklin helped the Apache spread the loose sand back over the corpse and then, without saying a word, Narsi walked to the horse he had ridden here and turned to look at Macklin.

"Keep it," said Macklin.

Narsi nodded, mounted and rode away. Some time would pass before Macklin saw him again.

Back at camp, Sterling was sitting, staring into the fire.

Macklin said, "You want to talk about this?"

Sterling seemed to have recovered to some degree. He said, "It's nothin'. I was a little surprised is all. Just a little surprised."

"Sure," said Macklin, but he was unconvinced.

After the discovery of Pete's body, Macklin's friendship with Sterling changed. The kid became uncommunicative and morose. The two men had never gotten to be close friends; there had always been a reserve in the kid—a wall that he kept between them, but at least he had been a somewhat congenial riding companion.

Macklin believed the kid was hiding something, and he guessed it had something to do with Pete. The core of the matter was that Macklin simply did not trust the kid anymore. And he did not want to ride with a man he didn't trust.

And so, having made this decision, he told Sterling one morning during breakfast, "I guess I'll be movin' on."

Sterling looked surprised. "To where?"

"I don't guess it matters much, does it?"

"Not much," said Sterling, and Macklin could tell the kid was angry.

Sterling said, "Did I do somethin' you didn't like, Macklin?"

"Fact is, you did a lot of things I didn't like, but there's no point in talkin' about them."

"I thought I was doin' you a favor, ridin' with you and all."

"I don't know what you were doing," said Macklin. "It always seemed to me like you had your own plan goin' on in your head. I figure on ridin' alone from here on out."

"Suits me right down to the ground," said Sterling, throwing half a cup of coffee into the fire. He rose and stalked away.

But there was something Macklin wanted to know, and he decided to take a chance. "There's something else, too, Sterling. I know about you and Pete."

Sterling spun around, reaching for his pistol.

But Macklin already had his out. He nodded. "I thought so."

Sterling gazed at him, and his face assumed a sneer. "You're a fool, Macklin. You'll never own half of Star. The only part of Star you'll ever get will be six feet deep by two feet wide." He spun on his heel, rolled his bedroll, gathered up his few belongings, and rode away.

Macklin watched him go, feeling disgusted with the whole situation. "Now," he muttered to himself, "would be a good time to go to Oregon." The thought was appealing, and he tried to talk himself into it, but he knew he would stay.

Sterling was right: he was a fool. Why, he asked himself, was he doing it? He had made a deal with Eli Nolan, but Eli was dead, and Tony would never honor his father's promise. Not now, after all that had happened. Why then did he stay? There was only one reason, and it was Tony Nolan.

It had occurred to Macklin that Pete was the man who had done the hiring on Star for some time. The more he thought about it, the more convinced he became that Pete had been crooked, and that he had placed at least one of his own men on the crew—a man who knew what Pete was planning. And whatever that was, he must have been planning it for some time. Things were starting to take shape in Macklin's mind, but he needed more information.

Finally, feeling depressed and more than a little discouraged, he decided to go to Benson for supplies and to enjoy a few of the comforts of civilization. He could use a bath, a shave, and a soft bed. He had thought of going to Contention City, where he had friends, but they all believed he was in Oregon, and he simply wasn't ready to explain this mixed-up situation he had gotten himself into—at least not until something was resolved one way or another.

It was after dark when he arrived in Benson, having picketed his pack mule outside of town. The barbershop was closed, but he rode to the saloon for a drink and that cigar he had been promising himself. He lingered at the door for a few moments, scanning the interior, never forgetting he was a man with enemies.

The barroom was full of men, but he saw none he recognized. He walked up to the bar and asked for a drink, keeping his eye on the mirror. It wasn't long before he saw a familiar face and its owner was walking toward him.

Neal Sterling was already moderately drunk, and he walked up to the bar and stood next to Macklin. "I wish you'd leave me alone," Sterling said.

Macklin turned to face him, saying nothing.

"Ain't you got nothin' to say to your old ridin' pardner?" said Sterling.

"Not a thing."

"Too bad." Sterling was not sober enough to be quick, and Macklin easily blocked the fist he swung and then knocked him flat on his back.

Sterling started to pull himself to his feet, but Macklin put his boot on the kid's chest as he tried to rise. "Stay down, Sterling. You're too drunk to fight."

Macklin downed his drink and left the barroom. In the darkness, he didn't notice the four Double H riders who rode in as he was untying his horse, nor did they see him. He went to a restaurant and had a good meal, and, as he was leaving, a man walked up to him and said, "Don't know if it matters to you, but that kid you fought with a while ago is in some bad trouble."

"Where?"

"The saloon where you fought him. Four Double H riders have him backed against the wall."

Macklin jumped into the saddle and spurred the horse down the street. He left the saddle on the run and dropped the reins while the horse was still moving. Sterling was just inside, standing next to the door, his hand on his gun butt, crouched slightly, every muscle as tense as a clock spring.

Macklin stepped through the doorway and this put him next to Sterling, who was facing four grinning Double H riders, one of whom was Floyd Colbert, the Double H foreman. Macklin did not look at Sterling, but he could hear the kid's heavy breathing and sense his fear.

Macklin had ridden long enough with Sterling to know the kid was not a coward, but he also knew that very few men could face almost certain death without feeling fear.

Floyd Colbert had been the only Double H survivor of the gunfight at Sally Pennington's party on the night Frank Doyle had been killed, and he had a healthy respect for Dave Macklin. On the other hand, he had three of his men backing him tonight.

He said, "You got no hand in this game, Macklin, and you're not the marshal here. You'd best stay out of it."

Macklin said, "Why don't you take your boys and go back to the ranch, Colbert? No point in people getting killed here."

"Your friend here was shootin' off his mouth, talkin' some pretty bold talk. Callin' us rustlers. A man needs to pay for that sort of thing. Ought to be able to back up his talk."

"He's drunk."

"Don't matter, Macklin. Man talks that way to me, he pays for it. I don't take that kind of talk from nobody. Now, you just step out of this. No need gettin' yourself carried out of here feet first."

Macklin took a stride forward, bringing him closer to Colbert. "I won't be the only one goin' out of here feet first."

Macklin's message was clear. At this distance, there was no way a man could miss. Regardless of whoever else got killed, he intended to make sure Colbert was among the dead.

The room was completely silent. A few tense moments passed, and Macklin said, "Anytime you're ready, friend, go ahead and let 'er rip." He was suddenly aware that Sterling was standing next to him.

Colbert's smugness had vanished. Macklin said, "I'll tell you what: Me and my pardner will just back on out of this room and be on our way. You boys can have your drinks, and we'll pretend like none of us ever almost killed each other."

Macklin could tell by Colbert's face that he had won. There would be no gunfight tonight. True to his word, he backed out of the room, and Sterling, beside him, did the same. Outside, as Macklin stepped into the saddle, Sterling, now reasonably sober, said, "There's a big barn just as you're comin' into town. Will you wait for me there?"

"Why should I?"

"No good reason, but I figure you will."

"Life's full of disappointments."

But Macklin, having retrieved his pack mule, was waiting by the barn, just as Sterling had predicted. The two men rode a few miles out into the desert and made camp. Macklin still had a little bacon and some flour and coffee. In the morning, he planned to return to Benson for his bath and haircut and to purchase supplies.

Without being asked, Sterling fixed supper, saying, "I figure it's my turn." After they had eaten, he said without preamble, "Pete was my old man. I never knew him until a few weeks before I met you. I didn't know anything about him until just before my mother died. She told me his name and that he was the foreman of Star Ranch, near Benson. After she died, I sent a letter to Benson for Pete Sterling of Star Ranch, and he wrote me back. He asked me to come out to Arizona but not to tell anybody who I was just yet. We met in Benson, and he acted real glad to see me. He told me that when Eli died, he and I were going to own Star."

"And what about Tony?" asked Macklin with a hard edge in his voice.

"Pete said Tony wasn't any good at runnin' a ranch and never would be. He said we'd look after him. He'd always have a place on Star. He'd be better off that way, because if he ran the ranch it would soon go bust and then he'd have nothin'. He said we'd be doin' Tony a favor."

"But you were going to have to kill some people to make all that happen," said Macklin.

"I didn't . . . I didn't think about that. I didn't know about it. Pete didn't tell me everything. One thing I never understood was the deal he made with a rancher named Doyle to rustle Star beef. I don't know why he did that."

"I do," said Macklin. The whole sordid plan was taking shape in his mind. Eli had told him there had been some Star riders who had been killed by the rustlers. Pete had needed a way of getting rid of members of the Star crew who he knew would oppose him—old, loyal Star hands who were a threat to him. He would send them to some distant part of the range and somehow get word to Doyle, telling him where they would be. Doyle and his men would wait in ambush and kill them.

A war against rustlers would provide Pete with all the excuses and opportunities he needed to enable him to take over Star and probably even a way to make it look legal. But the rustlers had gotten out of hand. They had taken more cattle than had been agreed upon. They must have started to act unmanageable, and Pete had gotten worried. He had helped Macklin escape, hoping Macklin could put some fear into the rustlers and at the same time protect Sterling, his son.

The whole thing sickened Macklin. He said, "Who killed Art and Dwayne and Nick?"

"I don't know. Maybe it was Pete's man on the crew."

"Who was that?"

"He didn't tell me. And, Macklin, I swear I didn't know there would be killings."

"That was part of the deal," said Macklin, "and you knew it."

"No. I didn't know it. I know it now, but I didn't know it then. I was supposed to keep a close eye on you, just in case you started to cause us trouble, and I did that. But then Pete got killed, I . . ."

"You didn't know what to do with me then, did you?"

Sterling looked at the ground. "I never could have killed you, Macklin. I—"

"Sterling, you'd better decide what kind of man you want to be. Because what you decide right now will determine the rest of your life."

"I have decided. I decided back there in the saloon, when you came in and stood beside me against Double H. I decided I want to be like you."

Neal Sterling was a different person after his candid talk with Macklin. Gone was the sullen, secretive person, whom Macklin had never trusted; replaced by a cheerful young man who sang and whistled and talked—sometimes a little too much for Macklin's liking—and who was as pleasant a riding companion as Macklin had ever known.

Sterling even shaved off his beard. He seemed to be no longer trying to look and act older than he was. It struck Macklin that the kid acted like someone who had been released from prison; and he realized that, in a sense, such was the case. Macklin thought he understood the kid now. He had grown up without a father and then, when he had reached manhood, he suddenly had one. And the man had promised his son they would have a good life together. Sterling had wanted this very much. He had wanted to please his father. And, though the things Pete had asked of him had gone against his nature, he had tried to go along with them. And then, after Pete's death, Sterling had become sullen and confused, no longer having any direction for his life.

It was a sorry thing, thought Macklin, when a man died and his son was better off because of it.

Sally Pennington's canned oysters arrived—boxes and boxes of them—and the manifold preparations for the party were begun, including arranging to have large quantities of fresh milk delivered on the day of the party, and ice to keep it from spoiling. Sally Pennington and her entire company, including Nan and Mandy and Todd, were kept busy for days with the business of the party. Even Milton was given some chores to do, and Mandy was to make sure he did them correctly.

The town had an ever-changing population and so, on the day of the party, there were a good number of new faces present, while some of the old, familiar ones were absent.

One of the new faces was that of Lena Carlson. She walked in, wearing the expensive blue dress Nan had given her, looking very self-conscious, made more self-conscious by the eyes that were turned upon her. Nan rushed over and whispered to her, "You are without a doubt the most beautiful woman here."

Lena blushed. "No, that would be you."

"Let's not call for a vote. I'm afraid I'd lose."

Children were never invited to Sally's parties, but an exception had been made for Mandy and Todd, who had become almost a part of the household. They had been told they had to stay in the kitchen but were given permission to eat as much as they wanted of anything there was to eat.

Marshal Belmont, thin and somewhat pallid, arrived, and Sally said to him, "Marshal, if you don't put back some of your weight tonight, I will consider my party to have been a failure."

"Mrs. Pennington, I wouldn't want to be the cause of any disappointment to you. I'll do my best."

Captain Paul Bitner was there, looking dashing as usual in his finest uniform.

During the first part of the party, Nan and Sally were kept busy greeting guests as they arrived, scurrying to and fro, helping the house staff, making sure everything was as perfect as possible. But after a while, things settled down, and they were able to casually move from group to group, engaging in polite conversation.

Eventually, Nan, exhausted from all this activity, found a chair in a corner and sat, content to observe from a distance. Presently Paul Bitner came over to her, as she had known he would, and said, "Care for a stroll in the garden?"

Nan forced a smile and rose. He took her arm, and they walked outside. It was a pleasant night but a little chilly, and she wished she had brought a shawl.

They strolled and chatted casually about unimportant subjects, then he led her to a bench in a far corner and they sat. The moon was bright, and he could see her features clearly. She did not look at him when he turned to face her. He put his arm around her and felt no give in her shoulders, no leaning against him. These were signs that Bitner understood well, and so, presently, he removed his arm and clasped his hands in front of him. Turning to face her, he said, "Is there someone else in your life, Nan?"

She dropped her eyes, "No."

"But it will never be me, will it?"

She turned to face him. "I'm sorry, Paul, I—"

"Please don't apologize. You have no reason to. You never led me on. I just hope we can always be good friends."

"Yes, Paul," she said. "I want that very much."

Something occurred to him at that moment. Something he had thought of in the past. Watching her features, which were almost as clearly seen in this bright moonlight as if it were day, he said, "I guess you heard about Dave Macklin?"

"You mean that he went to Oregon?"

"Oh, then you haven't heard. No, he never did go to Oregon. He went over to be the foreman of the Star Ranch."

Nan tried to disguise her feelings, but it was a vain attempt, and that night when the party was over and Bitner was riding away, he said to himself, "That son-of-a-gun. He got me back after all."

"Lot of dust over to the west," said Sterling. He had just come down from the hill from which he had been scanning the surrounding area while Macklin made the coffee for their lunch.

"Stagecoach?" asked Macklin.

"Too much dust, and then it cleared out."

Macklin set the coffee pot on a flat rock away from the fire, gave it a last longing look, and said, "We'd better go have a look."

A half hour later, approaching the road, they saw a man on foot. He waved them over, and when they came up to him, he said, "I wonder if you gents could come give us a hand. The stage to Tucson turned over down the road a ways. We need help settin' it back on its wheels."

"Sure," said Macklin, "Anybody hurt?"

"Just some scrapes and bruises."

It was not an uncommon occurrence for a stagecoach to overturn on these roads. Competing stage lines were advertising increasingly shorter times for the ride between Tombstone and Tucson and Tombstone and Benson, and drivers had to take risks in order to keep those increasingly impractical promises. On this occasion, the driver had taken a curve too fast and swerved too wide. The outside wheels slipped off the narrow road, and the stage slid into a shallow wash where it now rested on its side.

The passengers were all nearby, most of them sitting in the shade of a mesquite tree, and Macklin realized with a shock that one of them was Nan. She gave him a curt nod as he tipped his hat to her. Macklin and Sterling got their ropes on the coach, and, with the driver and the male passengers lifting, the coach was righted. Using the same combination of horsepower and manpower, it was pulled back onto the road, and the team was re-hitched.

Macklin stood by the door of the stage, assisting the women up the steps. When Nan's turn came, he asked her how she was. She replied coolly, "Very well, Mister Macklin, thank you."

"I suppose," he said, "you're surprised to see me here."

"Not at all. Mrs. Pennington and I had already learned you were not being truthful when you told us you were going to Oregon." Before he could say anything, she stepped into the coach.

CHAPTER 7

It wasn't until they shifted their search to the opposite end of the range—the north end—that Macklin and Sterling found the route the rustlers were using. But this was perplexing to Macklin. He said, "Why would they use this end of the range when it's so much farther to the border from here?"

Sterling said, "Maybe they ain't drivin' 'em to Mexico."

"Maybe not."

For hours, they followed the trail they had found, eventually coming to a place where clear signs on the ground showed this to be the spot where the rustlers had been rebranding the cattle. It was getting dark, so they moved a good distance away from the trail and made camp. The next morning, they returned to the branding site and continued to follow the trail. Macklin very much wanted to know where the trail of the stolen cattle led from this point.

It was late in the day when they arrived at a point that overlooked a small valley which held a house and a pole corral. Eight or ten horses were grazing nearby. In the fading light, smoke could be seen issuing from the chimney of the house. One woman and several men were visible, some sitting indolently on the porch in front of the house, and some wandering aimlessly about. The woman was washing clothes in a tub.

"It's an old mining claim," said Macklin. "See the dump pile over there?"

"Yeah, but those ain't miners down there."

"Nor law-abiding citizens either."

"So what do we do now?" asked Sterling. "What's your plan?"

Macklin looked at him and grinned. "The plan has two parts."

Sterling grinned back. "I know: The first part is to stay alive, and the second part you ain't figured out yet."

They had ridden a considerable distance from the outlaw's hideout before Macklin said, "Let's make camp." While they were eating, he said, "It's pretty clear it's the Double H that's doin' the rustling and the rebranding, and then they turn the cattle over to whoever is livin' in that valley." He was pensive for a moment, and then he exclaimed, "Why, I'll bet that's Owen Meeker's old gang. Sure, that's who it is, I'd bet a month's pay on it."

"You ain't drawin' any pay," said Sterling with a chuckle.

Macklin chuckled too. "Pretty sorry situation all the way around, ain't it?"

The next morning at breakfast, Macklin said, "How well do you know Tony Nolan?"

"Not very well. We only talked a few times. Seems like a decent sort."

"Let's hope he'll listen to us before he tells his boys to loosen up their ropes."

Macklin had just finished saddling his horse when the report of a rifle shot echoed across the little valley where they had camped. He heard the thud first and knew what it was. Spinning around, he saw Sterling on the ground next to his own horse, attempting to rise. The rifle report came again, kicking up dust just in front of Macklin. He saw the puff of smoke on the side of a distant hill as he jerked his carbine from the saddle scabbard. He dived to one side just as the shooter fired again. "Stay down and play dead," he shouted to Sterling.

He began firing at the spot where he had seen the puff of smoke. It was too far for accuracy: the shooter had chosen a bad place and had been lucky to hit Sterling with his first shot. Macklin's intent was to keep the man pinned down while Sterling found cover. "Can you move?" he shouted to the kid.

"I think so," said Sterling, his voice trembling.

"Crawl over here. I'll keep him busy."

The shooter had to expose himself a little in order to fire, and Macklin watched him and sent several bullets at him every time he did. Meanwhile, Sterling dragged himself along the ground, grunting in pain, finally making it to the spot where Macklin stood. Macklin set the carbine down and hoisted the kid into the saddle, quickly pulling the horse around a bend in the trail, where he and Sterling would not be exposed to the shooter. In doing so, however, he inadvertently provided opportunity to a second shooter who began firing at them.

"Get out of here!" He screamed at Sterling, and he slapped the horse hard. His last view of Sterling was of the young man slumped in the saddle, weakly kicking the horse in the flanks.

Macklin was aware that neither of the shooters was close, and he figured the best way to take advantage of that fact was to keep moving. He ran to the other horse and leaped into the saddle, barely conscious of the bullets flying past him. The carbine was lying on the ground where he had set it, and his six shooter and shell belt were still lying on his bedroll where he had left them when he went to saddle his horse. But he knew that to try to retrieve either weapon would probably be a fatal mistake.

He was unarmed.

Once in the saddle, he spurred the horse hard in the only direction that was available to him now, and it was opposite the direction in which he had sent Sterling. Within a short time, he was out of range of the shooters, but he knew he would be followed.

He wished there had been time to discuss a rendezvous point with Sterling. As it was, he had no way of knowing where the young man would go or how badly he was wounded. He took a few seconds to check his back trail. When he did, he could see the dust of his pursuers.

Two hours later, he could still see their dust, and a short time after that, from a high point in the trail, he was able to determine their number. There were three of them with one pack horse, and they were pursuing him with great determination.

All day long they followed him, and when night came he could still hear them behind him and, at times, when the wind was right, even smell their dust. Though Macklin was the one being pursued, he had had little choice in the trail he had chosen. The terrain and the closeness of his pursuers had dictated the direction he took.

Just after dark, he drastically changed his direction of travel in order to throw the men off his trail. Shortly afterward, he found a trail and gave the horse its head. The trail soon began sharply ascending.

Riding a horse in the dark has its inherent risks, but Dave Macklin had no other choice. It was about nine o'clock when the horse slipped on the steep, rocky trail and went down, falling on Macklin's right leg. It was all Macklin could do to keep from screaming from the pain.

The horse struggled to its feet, and when Macklin tried to do the same, his right leg nearly buckled under him. His knee was badly injured, he could tell.

With difficulty, he got back on the horse, only to find the animal was limping badly, favoring a front leg. There was nothing to be done for it now. He had to keep moving.

Macklin didn't care where the trail led, as long as he put as much distance as possible between himself and the men who were hunting him like an animal. He was no longer worried that they were behind him; they could not possibly have followed him in the dark.

Despite the pain in his knee, he found it hard to focus his mind. He had been in the saddle all day, and fatigue and pain had worn him out. The darkness soothed him, and he frequently caught himself dozing off. Finally, confident he was no longer being pursued, he decided to stop and rest.

He left his horse saddled and tied to a bush, and in the darkness he lay on the ground. It was only a short time before he began hearing hoof strikes on the trail below. He got up immediately and limped over to his horse and struggled into the saddle, wondering how the Double H men had followed his trail in the dark.

He found his answer less than a mile up the trail in the form of a small shack. This was undoubtedly a line shack used by the the Double H. Inadvertently Macklin had taken the same trail they would naturally take when finding themselves overtaken by nightfall in this part of the range. They had probably lost his trail and decided to call it a day when it got too dark for tracking. There would be bunks and food in the shack.

Macklin climbed off his horse and limped inside. He wanted to strike a match so he could look around, but he knew that if he did the men who were hunting him would smell it when they got here.

The shack was tiny; just large enough for a lower and upper bunk on either side, leaving not enough space between them for even a deal table. Nor was there a fireplace; the men would have to do their cooking outside. It was probably an old miner's shack that had been fixed up for use as a line shack. All over this desert, there were abandoned diggings and houses and shacks.

In the darkness, Macklin felt his way around, finding nothing in the way of guns or ammunition. There were some cans of food in a box nailed to the wall, and, unable to see the labels in the dark, he blindly took as many of these as he could carry.

When morning came, the men who were following him with such determination would—he had no doubt—see his tracks and renew the chase. By then he would have had all night to put as much distance as possible between him and them—though he worried about how he would do that on a lame horse. The last thing he wanted tonight was for them to become aware of the fact that he was just a short distance ahead of them.

Stuffing the cans into his saddlebags, he climbed into the saddle and proceeded up the trail, trusting—because he had no other choice—in the instincts, senses, and judgement of his horse. Soon, he knew, the moon would be out, and he would be able to see better and hopefully orient himself as to his location.

The horse was limping worse now, and Macklin climbed down and checked its leg, finding the ankle to be extremely swollen. The animal needed rest and its ankle needed attention, but those needs would have to wait.

A half mile up the trail, a dark form loomed ahead, and the horse stopped dead still. Macklin climbed down and limped forward and found that here the trail ended. The darkness in front of him was the sheer face of a hill or a mountain.

The best thing to do, he decided, was to wait for the moon to come out. He sat, leaning back against the mountainside, and soon dozed off. Presently he became aware of light coming through his closed eyelids.

He looked around in the light of the moon and saw the headframe of an old mine, and he instantly knew where he was. He had been here many years ago, before this mine had been abandoned.

Along with the discovery of where he was came the realization that he was in a worse predicament than he had previously realized. There was only one way down off this mountain, and that was the way he had come. There was nowhere to go but back down the trail that passed within a few feet of the little shack. And that shack, at this moment, held four killers who wanted him dead.

A man on foot, if he knew how to walk silently, could pass unheard, but a horse could not, yet Macklin knew that to allow daylight to find him still on this mountain would be fatal. Even if he could slip past undetected, where would he go on a lame horse? His pursuers would undoubtedly pick up his trail in the morning and follow.

He pulled himself to his feet and found that his knee had stiffened up during his brief rest, and when he checked it he found it to be swollen to almost twice its normal size. "We sure are a pair," he said to the horse as he checked its bad ankle.

He rode very slowly back down the trail, back toward danger; a lame man without a gun, riding a lame horse. When the line shack came into view below him, he was able to see in the bright moonlight that there was no light coming out of the crack around the door frame. These men, like himself, had ridden all day and it was late. He felt safe in assuming they were sound asleep.

The shack, being too small to stack saddles inside, had a rack on the wall outside. These men, though they were rustlers and killers, were also cowmen, and they never went anywhere without a lariat tied to the saddle.

Their horses would be picketed somewhere nearby, but Macklin could barely walk. And even if he could, roping a horse and saddling it would be a process that would make far too much noise. The situation seemed hopeless.

Dave Macklin had always been resourceful. He had once overheard his father tell someone, "If that boy can't figure out a way to do a thing, it just can't be done."

Those words came back to him now.

It was the time—a couple of hours after midnight—when the human energies are at their lowest ebb, and sleepers are in their deepest slumber. Otis Claxton, formerly of Texas, rider for the Double H outfit, rustler, outlaw, and implacable killer, was awakened. He thought he had heard a noise, a scuffing sound outside—a small animal perhaps.

He lay there for a while, listening to the heavy snoring of the other two men in the room. Whatever he had heard had not awakened them. He closed his eyes and was just drifting back into slumber when he felt movement beneath him. The line shack was moving. Was this an earthquake?

It became more pronounced. The shack was sliding. How could this be possible? Claxton jumped up, yelling. He hit the door with his shoulder, but it wouldn't open. He kicked the door. It did not budge. He was barely aware of the confused shouts of the other men in the shack.

Now the shack tilted, sliding faster. It was falling apart. Part of the roof fell in, hitting Claxton on the back and shoulders. The door flew open, but the bunk had fallen in front of him and he was pinned to it by the weight of the roof. He knew the terrain around the shack. He knew where the slope ended and what was there. The knowledge terrified him.

Claxton fought to free himself so he could get to the doorway and would have made it had not one of the other men pushed him aside in his own effort to get out. For a moment, the two men struggled, cursing each other savagely.

Then the grating sounds the shack had been making as it bumped and slid along the ground ceased. It rolled sideways, and the floor fell away. And Claxton felt nothing beneath him but air.

⌒◡◡⌒

Dave Macklin was not a man much given to self-recrimination, but the following morning as he stood on the edge of the canyon and surveyed the wreckage below, he couldn't help being sickened by the thought of what he had been forced to do. He had cut up his long underwear to make boots for his horse to soften the sound of its hoof falls. He had then crept to the shack, Apache style, and fastened the door from the outside with the leather thong that was there to keep rodents out. He had tied the men's lariats end to end and looped this long rope around the base of the shack, hitching the free end around his saddle horn, grateful the whole time, for the loud snoring of the men inside the shack.

Using the strength of his horse to pull the little shack off the narrow, flat area where it was situated, he slid it down the slope to where its own momentum took over, and then he let go of the rope.

Sickened by the screams of the men inside, Macklin watched in the bright moonlight as the shack went over the edge and disappeared into the darkness of the deep canyon.

In the fading light of the previous day he had passed a place where there was water. Mounted on the horse of one of the dead rustlers, he rode there and made camp. It was not the best of camping spots, but it would have to do until his knee healed, or he ran out of food.

Cliff Doyle rode over to the little valley where Lukert and his gang had their hideout. It took him nearly two hours to get there, and when he did he was hungry. Doyle and Lukert walked a short distance from the house, where they could speak in private. The outlaw said, "What's goin' on, Doyle? You're slowin' up on me."

"We're just havin' a little trouble, that's all. We'll get it taken care of."

"What kind of trouble?"

"Nothin' you need to worry about," said Doyle.

"My men are gettin' restless. Some of them are talkin' about leavin'. I think that's somethin' I need to worry about without you or anybody else tellin' me not to."

"All right, all right, Lukert. Don't get all heated up. Some things has happened that we wasn't expectin', that's all. But don't worry, we can take care of our end of things. I just rode over to let you know it might be a week or two before I send you another herd.

"Meanwhile me and my boys sit around here playin' cards and smellin' each other's sweat. Maybe I picked the wrong outfit to partner with. Send me some cattle, Doyle, and cut the excuses. You promised you could keep us busy. You said you could send us all the cattle we could handle. You'd better deliver, or we'll have to end this deal."

Doyle's face reddened and rough words came into his throat, but he held his tongue. From the very beginning, he had hated Lukert. Never had he allowed anyone to talk to him the way the outlaw leader did. During his adult life, he had never answered to any man except his brother. The two of them had been the bosses, and a man disrespected them at his own peril. But Lukert seemed to know how much Doyle needed him and his men. Doyle was new in the area and had no contacts outside of Lukert's outlaw band. Rustling cattle was one thing, but finding a market for the stolen animals and evading the law while doing it were different matters altogether.

Eventually, Doyle intended to take over this entire range—Star Ranch included—and when he did, he would have no more need for Lukert and his crew. But for now he was obligated to put up with whatever Lukert dished out. He said, "This ain't as easy as it might seem to you, Lukert. Star is a big ranch, they've got a sizable crew, and they're fightin' hard. We've got the situation in hand, but I'm tellin' you, I won't have any beeves for you for a week or two, that's all."

"All right, Doyle, I guess for now I have to take it, but I don't have to like it." Lukert turned and walked back to the house, indicating by this that the conversation was over and Doyle was dismissed. Having expected to be fed, Doyle was forced to make the long ride back to the ranch with an empty stomach and a chest full of rage.

"Milton is so happy these days," said Sally to Nan. "I always used to wonder if he saw himself as a child or an adult. But he always seemed so gloomy in adult company. It's clear to see that he really does enjoy acting like a child."

Mandy and Todd had been coming over almost daily to take advantage of Sally Pennington's library. Mandy in particular enjoyed the books, and Sally allowed her to take one home when she wished. Mandy loved the ones about faraway places, especially when there were illustrations, and she was inordinately fond of Mrs. Pennington's atlas.

But they did more than read at Sally's house. Mandy and Todd and Milton sometimes spent hours playing teetotum, dominoes, or jackstraws. Jackstraws were Mandy's favorite, and Sally had a set of ivory ones.

"He does seem happier than I've ever seen him," agreed Nan, referring to Sally's comment on Milton's recent demeanor. "And the children don't seem to care that on the outside he's a middle-aged man."

"And have you noticed that Mandy just naturally seems to take charge and act like a little mother hen?"

"Yes. She's definitely the one in charge."

"She's not so much bossy as she is protective," said Sally. "I wish I'd thought of this a long time ago."

Macklin stayed in his hidden camping spot for more than a week, allowing his knee to heal, rationing out the food he had taken from the ill-fated line shack, allowing himself only a small amount each day. He had made a splint for his leg out of sticks and braided cords he made of hairs pulled from his horse's tail. He had found another stick, a longer one, which he had made into a crutch, and he stayed off the leg as much as possible.

After a week, his knee was much improved, and he was out of food. He needed supplies, and he needed a gun and some ammunition. Too, he was worried about Sterling and he wanted to try to find the kid.

He rode back to the place where Sterling had been shot, picked up his trail, and followed it, finally arriving at a point where the kid had fallen from his horse. Here there was a significant amount of blood and a long smear that showed where Sterling had dragged himself into the shade of a paloverde tree. But Sterling was not there, and there was no sign to tell Macklin where the kid had gone. Macklin, however had his suspicions. At any rate, the kid was beyond his help.

It was late when Clara left to go home. Doctor Pope had repeatedly cautioned her against going out after dark in this town, telling her it was unsafe for a woman alone, even in daylight. Clara, however, was accustomed to ignoring the doctor's warnings. She had walked home many times in the dark and had no reason to think this time would be any different.

Lem Trainor had noticed Clara before and thought her to be a fine-looking woman. He had heard she was a widow, and in his egotistical mind, this fact left the door open for a man like him.

If Lem had known what Clara thought of men like him, he would not have been so optimistic about his chances. He was a ne'er-do-well who spent most of his time in the seedy establishments on the rough side of town. He thought of himself as a fast gun, and indeed, had killed two men in stand-up gunfights. He drank to excess, seldom bathed, and made his living—such as it was—by cheating at cards.

Tonight Lem Trainor was more than half drunk and was walking down the street toward his favorite saloon when he saw Clara walking toward him. They were in a dark area where there was a break between buildings. Trainor looked around, and seeing there was no one nearby, reached out as she walked past, grabbed hold of her arm, and pulled her to him. She started to scream, but he smashed his mouth onto hers and held her head so she could not escape his violent kiss.

When she broke free from his grip, she stumbled and fell backward, landing in the dirt. He laughed and reached down, offering to help her up, but she screamed and pulled herself to her feet and ran away.

***

Owen Meeker spent his time alternately resting and practicing with his guns. He knew he wasn't ready yet for what was to come, but he soon would be. He slept a lot and ate restaurant food, remembering the sumptuous meals Dr. Pope's wife had prepared for him while he was under her husband's care. His thoughts often turned to Clara, and when they did, he felt the anguish of irretrievable loss.

Presently, feeling stronger, he rented a horse and rode to Contention City, intentionally arriving there well after dark. He rode to Doctor Pope's house and quietly slipped two envelopes under the front door. One of the envelopes contained enough money to more than pay for the services Meeker had received from the doctor. The other, addressed to Clara, contained an even larger sum of money— far more than the amount she had loaned him. This accomplished,

Meeker rode over to McDermott's Saloon and had a drink. It was there that he overheard two men talking about Clara Teel's encounter with Lem Trainor.

Trainor had been arrested for assault on a woman, and a hearing was scheduled before Major Clifton, who regularly donned his judicial robes and held court in the very saloon in which they were drinking at that moment.

～∾∾⌒

The hearing was a short one. Feeling uncomfortable in this barroom, Clara told her version of the story, and afterward, Lem Trainor was allowed to tell his version. He was well-dressed today, sober, and clean-shaven. He said, "Your Honor, I'm real sorry Mrs. Teel took offense at me kissin' her. I sure never meant no harm."

"Just tell us what happened, Mr. Trainor," said Major Clifton, the judge.

Well, I was walkin' down the street, and I saw her comin' toward me. I had seen her a few times before, and she always smiled at me and sometimes we talked—"

"That's a lie," interrupted Clara indignantly, "I never—"

"Mrs. Teel," said the judge, "you've had your time to talk, now let the accused have his." He nodded to Trainor.

"Well, Your Honor, she stopped and acted like she wanted to talk, so I stopped too. We visited for a while, and she asked me if I was married. I said I wasn't, and she said she wasn't either. Then she moved close to me. Real close, with her face turned up like a woman does when she wants a man to kiss her. I thought I understood what she was tellin' me." He looked at the judge and gave him a fraternal smile. "Well, Your Honor, I guess I'm like a lot of men: Whenever I think I understand what a woman is thinkin', she goes and proves me wrong."

There was a pause while the men in the room chuckled, some of them nodding commiseratively.

Trainor continued, "I feel real bad about the whole thing," and, turning to Clara, he said, "I'm sure sorry, Mrs. Teel. I know I offended you, and I'm sorry about your sprung wrist, but," turning back to the judge, "my only crime was not understandin' women.

160

And if you're going to start jailin' men for that, pretty soon there won't be any men left that ain't behind bars."

Almost all the men in the room, including the judge, laughed.

Clara didn't see Owen Meeker come into the room and sit in the back shortly after she made her statement. Nor did she see him leave immediately after the judge levied the five-dollar fine—with no jail time—against Trainor. In fact, Clara would never see Meeker again.

Owen Meeker walked into the barroom and stood in its center, looking around. When he saw the man he was looking for, he found a table nearby, sat down, and settled his gaze on the man. It was Lem Trainor.

Trainor soon became aware of the man looking at him, and he frowned his resentment. Meeker continued staring, and Trainor looked at him. "You see somethin' interestin' over here, Mister?"

Meeker continued staring.

Trainor pushed back his chair, stood up, and started to cross the distance between them, clearly intending to deal with this with his fists. But Meeker rose and stood by his table, his hand above his gun. There would no fist fight. Meeker had declared his intentions.

Trainor licked his lips and smiled a wicked grin, moving his hand toward his gun. Men moved away from the two, not wanting to catch a wild bullet. A man who had been sitting at the same table as Trainor said in a low voice, "Lem, that's Owen Meeker."

Lem Trainor was not a faint-hearted man, but few men can look death in the face with a smile. Lem's went away. After a long hesitation, during which there was almost no sound in the room, he decided to talk. "What do you want with me, Meeker? I never done you no harm."

Meeker made no reply. There was no change on his countenance. He kept his hand above his gun.

Sweat appeared on Trainor's face. His voice was unsteady. "You ought to tell a man what you got against him."

Meeker did not move.

For a few agonized seconds, Trainor stood there, watching the unchanging, faintly sneering face of the gunman. Finally, he moved his hand away from his gun, cursed, and turned away, his face flushed with resentment and humiliation. He walked to the door, violently thrust it open, and stepped outside. In his distracted and angry state, he bumped into Milton, Sally Pennington's nephew, who was on an errand for his aunt.

Trainor was not drunk, but he had enough alcohol in him to repress good sense, and, added to that, he was ready to take out his anger and frustration on anyone he encountered. He cursed Milton and gave him a shove and then a vicious kick, sending him sprawling. "Stay out of my way," he bawled.

At that moment, Trainor was struck by a scratching, clawing, screaming ball of fury. Mandy was on him like a wildcat.

Infuriated beyond reasoning, Trainor swore at her and shoved her away. When she came back at him, he swung an open hand that connected with the side of her face—much harder than he had intended—sending her into the dust in a limp heap.

Bellowing curses at Milton and Mandy and the world in general, Trainor turned away and walked right into a huge fist that knocked him off his feet. He lay on his back, looking up at Bo Creech, who cursed him savagely and threatened him with sundry kinds of violence if he ever laid another hand on that girl.

Lem Trainor was having a bad day.

It was about to get worse.

It took a little time for Trainor's head to clear, and he did not attempt to rise until after Bo Creech picked Mandy up and took her in his arms and, with a murderous backward glance, carried her toward the doctor's place.

The scene had attracted a crowd. Two well-dressed women were berating Trainor for hitting a little girl. Passersby had stopped to watch, others had come out of stores and businesses, drawn by the shouting. It seemed to Trainor that the whole town had assembled to witness his humiliation. Remembering how it had all started, he pulled himself to his feet, gave a feral cry, and rushed back into the saloon, pulling his gun as he pushed through the door.

Owen Meeker had not moved. He was standing in the same spot he had been in when Trainor left the room. As Trainor rushed in, raising his pistol, Meeker drew his gun in a fluid blur.

And Lem Trainor's bad day came to a sudden and conclusive end.

"It was a fair fight," Dr. Pope said to Clara. "There were plenty of witnesses. They all said Trainor drew first."

"But why did he want to kill Owen?"

"Apparently Meeker provoked him."

"How? He can't even speak."

Dr. Pope looked down at the floor and shook his head in disgust. "He stared at him."

"What?" she asked incredulously.

"Meeker intentionally provoked him. He stared at him until Trainor took offense. There were words . . . well, Trainor said some words. Right then, nothing happened. Trainor went outside, and . . . I don't know exactly what happened there, but that was when Trainor hit the Carlson girl. Then Bo Creech laid Trainor out, and after that, Trainor went back inside the saloon and pulled his gun. Meeker shot him in self-defense."

"But Owen started it."

"That's one way of looking at it. The law looks at it as self-defense. There's no law against staring at someone."

"You know why he did it, don't you?"

"Listen, Clara. You can't blame yourself."

She shook her head and turned away, sick at heart.

"Wait, Clara."

She stopped but did not turn back to face him.

He said, "You saved a man's life. That was your job, and you did it well. You have no control over what he does with that life. You didn't know he was a gunman when he was brought here, and yet, if you had the whole thing to do over, you would—"

"Let him die," she interrupted. "If I had it to do over, I would let him die."

She walked away.

"Lukert says we'll be leaving here soon," said Phil. He and Julia were taking a walk, following their customary route, being careful to stay within sight of the man who had been assigned to watch them. The sun had dropped below the western rim of the canyon, and the shadows in the little valley were deepening.

"He's said that before," said Julia, "and we're still here."

"Everyone's getting restless, not just us."

"At least they're not stuck here all day long every day. They're not prisoners."

They stood leaning against the top rail of the corral, speaking in low, despondent tones. They were two people who were running out of hope. The man who was keeping an eye on them sat on a barrel chair by a corner of the house, idly smoking a cigarette. Had he been more alert, he could have perhaps prevented what happened next, but he had no reason to expect danger. A shadow moved to one side of him from out of the semidarkness, and, turning to look, the outlaw had just a moment—before the razor-sharp knife blade slid between his ribs and stopped his heart—to realize he was seeing a ghost.

Phil and Julia did not see what happened; they were facing another direction, and their thoughts were centered on other things. They stood there in depressed silence until a sound behind them made them turn. Julia gasped and lurched backward, coming up against a corral post. She would have screamed, but no sound would come out of her throat. Horrified, Phil shrank away from the apparition as Julia, her strength leaving her, sank to the ground.

"Owen," said Phil, the word coming out as a hoarse gasp. Then, seeing the pistol in Owen's hand, he said, "Please, no, Owen. Me, but not her. Don't hurt Julia." He put himself between Owen and Julia, shielding her with his body.

Owen stood looking at the two for a long, excruciatingly intense moment. Finally, he holstered the pistol, reached down, and took Julia by the hand, pulling her to her feet. The girl was trembling uncontrollably. Taking Phil's hand, Owen put it over onto Julia's in a symbolic gesture, then pulled a large envelope from inside his shirt and gave it to Phil. It was then that Phil noticed that Owen was wearing two pistols—one in the holster and one in his waistband.

Turning away now, Owen walked with his curious gait toward the house, and by the time he reached it he had a cocked pistol in each hand.

Lukert had lost interest in the poker game an hour or so earlier, and since then he had been steadily losing. The haze of smoke that filled the room and the fact that it was getting dark outside were making him sleepy. The door opened and someone came in. Assuming it was Hart, the man he had sent to keep an eye on Phil and Julia, Lukert gave him the briefest of glances, and then, with a gasp, he jerked his head back around to face the newcomer. It was then that hell erupted inside the room.

Outside in the darkness, Phil and Julia listened as the sounds of frenzied gunfire came from inside the house. Phil looked around for the man who had been guarding them, expecting him to be alerted by the gunshots, but the man was nowhere to be seen, and it came to Phil that Owen, of necessity, would have killed him first.

The gunfire was dying out now, the shots more widely spaced. There came one final shot, then silence.

"Stay here," Phil said to Julia, and ran toward the house.

"Be careful," she called after him.

Reaching the doorway, Phil halted, realizing it would not be a good idea to burst into the room. He said, "Don't anybody shoot, it's just me, Phil." The smell of gunpowder was strong in the doorway.

The lantern on the table was still glowing, though someone had knocked off the glass chimney. Owen was sitting on the floor, his back to the wall, blood pooling around him. His left hand was empty; his right hand, resting on the floor, still held a pistol. He was looking at Phil, following him with his eyes.

There were bodies all around the room, most of them sprawled on the floor, one still in a chair. One man, lying in a corner, was moaning softly; all the others appeared to be dead. Lukert had been shot once—in the head.

The moaning man said, "Help me, Phil. I'm hurt bad." Phil went to him, took a look at his wounds, and said, "Jack, you're a dead man."

Hearing a gasp behind him, Phil turned quickly. Julia was in the doorway. Phil said, "You don't need to see this, Honey. Wait for me outside."

Ignoring him, she went to Owen and knelt in front of him. "I'm sorry, Owen, I'm so sorry."

He looked at her with an expression in his eyes that she would never forget.

"Owen," she sobbed, "say something."

Almost imperceptibly, he shook his head, and then his eyes went blank.

～～～

It had been several weeks, and Macklin's knee was healed. He had ridden to Bisbee, where he had taken a room in a boardinghouse, giving himself and his horse time to mend. Now he was back in the desert, determined to find Sterling, or at least learn what had happened to the kid. And he knew right where to go for that information.

He picketed his horse and pack mule in a small valley and set up his camp nearby. Not far away was a prominent hill where he built a small fire, and, after tying his bandana to a nearby tree, he went back to his camp.

The following morning, while he was cooking breakfast, Narsi appeared in camp and sat cross-legged near the fire while Macklin fed him bacon, pan bread, and coffee.

After eating, the Apache stood and walked to his horse. Macklin followed him, and presently they were at a canyon, where, in a small cave, Narsi had been caring for Sterling.

Macklin was pleased to see the young man, but when he asked how he was doing, Sterling answered irritably, "How's it look like I'm doing? I've been shot, and I'm lyin' on the ground gettin' fed by an Indian."

Macklin glanced at Narsi, who, in a disgusted tone spoke the Apache word for baby.

"You ought to be glad you're alive," said Macklin.

"Pretty easy thing to say when you're walkin' around with no bullet holes in you."

Macklin had been raised to believe that self-pity was the most unmanly of emotions, and the kid's churlish whining irritated him. He was pensive for a moment and then said, "Years ago, when I was about fourteen, I was with a few of my friends, and we decided to round up some range cows and try to ride them. We were having a pretty good time, until one of them bucked me off and then turned around and charged me. I got a broken arm and some busted ribs out of it. I remember whining and complaining just like you are now, until one of my uncles came over to visit one day and said to me, 'Didn't you know it was dangerous to ride wild cows?'

"Well, of course I had to say yes to that, and he said, 'Didn't you know you might get hurt?' I said yes. Then he said, 'Sometimes I get drunk, and the next day I have a hangover. But I knew that would happen before I started drinkin', so I never complain about it.'"

Macklin paused for a moment and said, "After that I quit whining about my broken bones."

Sterling looked away, saying nothing, and Macklin said, "Before you stepped into this fight, kid, you knew it would be dangerous. You knew you might get shot at. A man takes his risks, and then he lives with what happens."

Without looking at Macklin, Sterling nodded.

Macklin said, "Narsi says you're going to be all right. That's good."

"Yeah, I guess it is," murmured Sterling.

As he was leaving the cave, Macklin said, "I brought some food. I'll be back in a week or so to see how you're doing."

Outside, Narsi said, "That was good talk. I thought only Indian smart like that."

Macklin returned a week later and found Sterling prepared to leave and Narsi glad to see him go. Macklin stayed overnight, and he and Narsi sat up late in conversation. They spoke in English and Apache, discussing the situation and deciding upon a plan.

The next day, Macklin and Sterling rode to the place where Macklin had been camping, arriving there after dark.

After supper, Macklin said, "Tomorrow I'm going to talk to Tony Nolan. I want you to stay here."

"You sure that's a good idea?"

"No, but it's the only idea I've got."

"How about the one about stayin' alive? That might not work so well if Tony's crew still has a notion to hang you."

"I'm hopin' they're over that sentiment. The thing is, Sterling, we've pretty much got things figured out now. The only thing we don't know is where they've been taking the cattle to sell them, and that part doesn't matter anyway."

Sterling nodded. "It's your funeral."

Tony Nolan sat despondently in his father's old chair and thought about the old days when he had been happy, before all this weight had been laid on his young shoulders. He felt very alone. True, he had his crew, but they were, for the most part, men he had only known for a short time. Most of the old hands had either been killed, had quit, or had been fired by Pete in the last few months before he disappeared. And, though he was young and inexperienced, Tony knew the hands Pete had hired to replace the old ones were not the kind of men he could rely on to help him win this war against the rustlers. Moreover, they had little confidence in him. He was not respected as his father had been, nor were his orders obeyed as his father's had been.

Eli had built this ranch, had carved it out of the wilderness, and now Eli was gone. Pete was gone too, and no one knew where he had gone or what had happened to him.

Everything in Tony's life had changed in just a short time. Time and again over the past few weeks, he had asked himself what his father would have done in this situation and had found no answer. It all seemed very hopeless.

He went to his room, pulled off his clothes, and lay on the bed. It was late when he finally went to sleep, and much later when a shadow materialized out of the darkness of the desert, moved silently to the back door, opened it, and slipped inside the house.

While Tony Nolan slept, Narsi set a folded paper on the kitchen table and slipped out of the house and back into the shadows.

The next morning when Tony awoke, he went to the kitchen for a drink of water. That was when he saw the folded paper.

He opened it and read the note written on it:

Tony.

Neal Sterling and I have figured out who is doing the rustling and where they are taking the cattle. Pete was in on it with them and they killed him. One of your riders is a traitor. I do not know who he is, but if you tell your crew you are going to throw in with me again, he will be the one that talks most against it. He will accuse me and Sterling of being killers. Watch your men closely and you'll be able to tell which one it is. He is working with your enemies. I want to help you,

Tony. Your father trusted me. That should mean something to you. I can only help you if you trust me too.
   Dave Macklin

Tony sat immobile for several minutes, holding the note in his hand. He re-read it and then carefully folded it and, after dressing, put it in his pocket. For some reason that he didn't completely understand, he did not question the note. He accepted that it was from Dave Macklin, and he accepted that what Macklin had written was true. Perhaps it was because he wanted to believe, to suddenly have hope again, to feel like he wasn't completely alone in a futile battle against an unknown enemy. But, whatever the reason, he felt enlivened. He finally had a plan.

After breakfast he assembled his crew and stood before them, as he knew his father would have done. He said, "Boys, I've received a message from Dave Macklin, and I've decided to join up with him. I don't think he's a killer, and we can use his help."

Most of the men made some sort of outward reaction to these words, some positive, some dissenting, but one man in particular, Tony's foreman, Max Holder, exploded, "You must be jokin', Tony. What are you tryin' to do to this ranch? Why, your father is rollin' around in his grave right now. Macklin's a murderer. All he wants is to steal the ranch from you."

And then Tony knew. And he wondered why it had taken him so long to figure it out. This man was a traitor. Of course he was. Tony pulled his gun and pointed it directly at Holder. He said, "Jeff, Bill, get his gun. He's a traitor."

"You sure about this?" said Bill.

Holder's demeanor changed instantly, and he became apparently docile. As rough hands took hold of him and took away his pistol, he said, "It's all right, boys. I won't fight you. This is just a big mistake."

And then, with animal quickness, he wrenched a hand free, siezed his pistol from the hand of the man who held it and swung it around, cocking it as he did.

Tony had already holstered his pistol, but now he instinctively lurched to one side as he pulled it out again. The move saved him. Holder's bullet passed by his head, taking away a small piece of his ear. A fraction of a second later Tony fired and Holder was thrown backward, landing on his back.

There were exclamations of shock and dismay, and Tony said, "Hold tight, Boys. I'm not through. Jeff, come here." He pulled the note from his pocket and handed it to Jeff, saying, "Read it out loud. You're my new foreman."

While some of the men attended to Holder, who was not dead, Jeff read the note. When he was finished, some of the crew members voiced doubt, while others saw the truth in Macklin's words.

Jeff Trapp, the new foreman, said, "I never felt right about Holder, and I never made no secret of it. He claimed to be from Missouri, but he talked like a Texan. He come from out of nowhere and Pete hired him over some men that had been on Star for a long time. It all stacks up now."

They took Holder into the bunkhouse and put him on a bunk. He was dying, and everyone knew it. One of the older hands squatted by the bunk and said, "Max, you're cashin' your chips today, and if there's anything you need to square up, you ought to be doin' it pretty quick. A man don't want to go out of this world carryin' all his sins with him. You'd be doin' us all a big favor if you'd shed the light on this business so we'll know which way to head when you're gone."

Max Holder gave a weak smile of irony and said with a voice that was so feeble as to be nearly inaudible. "It's all true. I worked for Double H. Pete made a deal with the Doyles. You can figure out the rest."

"Who killed Art and Dwayne and Nick Jason?"

"Pete," said Holder in a fading voice. He turned his head away and whispered, "Now leave me alone."

They left him there and later came back and wrapped him in the bloody blanket he was lying on and took him to the grave they had dug for him.

And from that day forth, Tony Nolan was the unquestioned master of Star Ranch.

<hr />

The day after the death of Max Holder, Macklin showed up at Star Ranch, just as Tony—who now took his meals with the crew—and his men were going to breakfast. Macklin had known he was taking a chance—Narsi had advised against it—but he knew instantly by the way the men regarded him as he rode into the yard, that their former hostile feelings toward him had eased to some degree. Not that he was welcomed warmly by the Star men—they had been betrayed too many times to merely accept him without suspicion—but at least they didn't immediately take him and hang him from the nearest barn rafter.

Tony Nolan walked over to him and said, "Howdy, Macklin."

Jeff Trapp came over and stood next to Tony, asserting his authority by this move.

Stepping out of the saddle, Macklin said, "Your new foreman?"

Tony nodded.

Macklin didn't ask what had happened to Max Holder, but he had his suspicions.

Tony said, "We want to talk to you, Macklin. Come on inside."

Old Eli's bed had been taken out of the front room, but otherwise everything was as it had been when Macklin had been here last. He was motioned to a seat next to a small table, and Tony sat opposite him. Jeff Trapp chose to remain standing.

Macklin pulled an envelope from inside his shirt and set it on the table, but before he could speak, Tony began, "You were right about the traitor, Macklin, but we still have some worries about you."

"Such as?"

Trapp stepped in at this point. "It just seems like you know way too much about what Star's enemies are up to."

Macklin resented the inference, resented Trapp's demeanor toward him, and, in view of the fact that this last was not phrased as a question, he said nothing. He did not look at Jeff Trapp or acknowledge him in any way. He sat gazing at Tony.

Trapp said, "Well?"

Macklin still did not respond.

"Now look here, Macklin. We need some kind of answer," demanded Tony.

"To what? I haven't heard a question yet."

"All right," said Trapp, "how about this: What do you want from Star? Because Eli's dead, and you ain't gettin' half the ranch like you're probably thinkin'"

Macklin said, "Who am I going to deal with, Tony? You, or your talking jackass here?"

At this, Trapp strode furiously across the room toward Macklin, who stood up and was waiting for him. Macklin took a punch on the side of the head while he drove three fast jabs into Trapp's midriff, bending the foreman over, then putting him on the floor with a hard right to the jaw.

Tony shouted, "All right, that's enough." He looked at Macklin. "It just seems like every time you come to Star, you stir up trouble. I think we can do better without you, Macklin."

Macklin picked up his hat and said, "Tony, you're young, and you can be excused for being a fool. But there's no excuse for him." He put on his hat and started toward the door. Turning back, he said, "Maybe you think you don't need me, Tony, but you'll never save this ranch without my help."

Trapp sat up, rubbing his jaw. "Your help? All you want is to steal the ranch from him. That kind of help he can do without."

Macklin pointed to the envelope on the table. "There it is, signed and witnessed. Keep your ranch, Tony, and enjoy it for as long as you can. It'll soon be gone, and I think you know it. I also think you know that Mule Face here," he pointed to Trapp, "won't be able do a single thing to stop that from happening."

He left the house, got on his horse, and rode away.

After Macklin was gone, Tony opened the envelope and removed the document it contained. He read it and then looked at Trapp.

"What is it?" asked Trapp.

"It says he legally gives up any claim to any part of Star. Like he said, it's signed and witnessed."

"Well, that's good, Tony," said Trapp. "That's a good thing."

Tony looked at him and shook his head. "Macklin's right, Jeff. We're a couple of fools."

Macklin was not as angry as he had acted. He had wanted to impress upon Tony's mind the facts he had stated, and, since Tony wouldn't put his foreman in his place, Macklin had seen fit to do so. He was glad Tony had a foreman who was protective of the young man and his interests, but he believed there could only be one headman, and that man needed to take charge; otherwise, things could get out of hand.

He had anticipated the suspicion Jeff Trapp had raised and for that reason had gone to the attorney in Charleston and paid him to draft and witness the document he had given to Tony.

Macklin had never been the kind of man who liked to get something for nothing. From the beginning, he had had reservations about accepting Eli Nolan's offer but had known that Eli and Tony needed his help—and he had been willing to give it. Later, when he had learned that Eli was dead, he had abandoned any thought of holding Tony to the promise.

But Eli had been a friend, and his son was in trouble. Macklin had promised he would help, and he intended to do so, even if he had to do it against Tony's wishes. He hoped, however, that would not be the case.

And so, riding away from Star, he rode slowly.

He was not more than a mile away from headquarters when he heard hoofbeats. He looked back. It was Tony.

Cliff Doyle was not happy with the recent turn of events. Three of his men—the three that had been sent to hunt down and kill Macklin and Sterling—had simply disappeared. He was certain they would return eventually, but for now, of the original crew Doyle and his brother had brought with them from Texas, there remained only three. One of them was Floyd Colbert, Doyle's foreman.

When Colbert returned from an unsuccessful scout to try and find the three missing riders, he reported having seen a sizeable herd of cattle on the south range of Star.

"Look like they're just waitin' for us," he told his boss.

"That's good," said Doyle, "Lukert's been chewin' nails waitin' for us to send him some more beeves."

Because of the diminished size of his crew, Doyle himself rode with his men to round up the cattle and drive them north to the re-branding site.

Doyle was not a young man, and he had been an outlaw all his life. He had not outlived his father and all his brothers, as well as more than a few uncles and cousins, by being careless. And now he feared a trap.

During the drive, he watched the country more than he did the cattle, frequently riding ahead to scout the trail, constantly alert for any sign of trouble. There was a place up ahead that he had always thought to be a perfect site for an ambush, and now, as the herd approached that spot, Doyle thought more and more that this felt like a trap.

He reined in his horse and signaled for his men to stop the herd. He sat there, torn between his need for caution and his need to provide Lukert and his gang with some cattle to sell, not knowing that neither Lukert nor any of his men would ever sell another beef—or anything else—again.

Doyle's caution won out. He said to Floyd Colbert, "Leave the cattle. We're gettin' out of here."

"You must be feelin' the same thing I'm feelin'," said Colbert.

They turned their horses toward their back trail, and the second they did, the surrounding hills erupted in gunfire.

Whipping and spurring their horses, they rode away, heading for a gap in the hills a few hundred yards away. They had almost reached it when Colbert, riding next to Doyle, suddenly slumped and fell out of the saddle.

The Star men pursued the three remaining Double H men without success, until darkness came, when they lost the trail. At that point, they rode straight for the Double H headquarters, arriving there at about midnight. They entered cautiously, but, except for several women, the place was deserted. Doyle had been too smart to return here.

Tony Nolan told the women to gather their belongings, and he ordered his men to hitch up a wagon for them. When the women were gone, Tony ordered the Star crew to burn every building, corral, and haystack at Double H.

As he watched the Double H burn, Macklin felt little satisfaction. He had been keenly disappointed by the failure of his well-planned ambush. He realized now that Doyle was more chary than he had thought. If the rustlers had continued forward another hundred yards with the stolen cattle, none of them would have escaped, but Doyle had stopped and sat there on his horse, almost like a deer sniffing the wind for a predator. And he had obviously decided not to take the risk.

The Star riders had shot at the fleeing rustlers, but the distance was too great for accuracy. It had merely been a lucky shot that had downed Floyd Colbert.

Well, thought Macklin, consoling himself, most of the Double H crew were dead, and the ranch headquarters were burned. Doyle and his two remaining men had not been hanged, but at least they would leave the area. There was nothing left for them here.

CHAPTER 8

"**I** want to talk to you, Macklin," said Tony.

The crew had arrived back at Star that afternoon, bringing a few head of horses they had found on the Double H. The weary men had just finished eating and were going to bed early. Macklin and Sterling had been offered a bunk for the night.

They went inside the house. Jeff Trapp went in with them and sat regarding Neal Sterling—who had not been invited to accompany them—with some disfavor. Over the past few days, Macklin and Trapp had forgotten their differences and become friends. Macklin still called him Mule Face, and Trapp was good-natured about it.

Seeing Trapp's face now as he looked at Sterling, Macklin said, "Neal, maybe you'd better wait outside."

It seemed to dawn on Sterling that he had come in uninvited, and he quickly rose and left the room.

Tony Nolan was a far different person than the young man Macklin had met that day in Contention City when Tony and his two riders had gone to bring him to meet with Old Eli. Since that night, Tony had been forced to shoulder a heavy load of responsibility. Macklin had noticed how the young man tried to sound tough and forceful and manly when he spoke to other men. One day, this demeanor would reflect the true man, but for now it seemed somewhat artificial, at times making Macklin want to smile.

It made him want to smile now, when Tony addressed him in his man-to-man voice. "Macklin, I want to talk to you about the agreement my father made with you before he died."

"That deal's off. I gave you the paper."

"That paper don't mean a thing to me. My Pa made you an offer, and I'm bound to honor his word. What I'm tellin' you is that half of Star is yours."

"Tony, I told your Pa I would help you when he was gone, but I never did tell him I accepted his offer. It was too much; too generous. I didn't feel good about it then, and I still don't."

Tony was thoughtful for a moment, and he said, "Jeff, I want to talk to Macklin alone."

The obedient manner in which Jeff Trapp accepted this told Macklin that Tony was truly in charge now.

When Trapp was gone, Tony's demeanor changed. His voice became that of a young man asking for help. He said, "Mr. Macklin, My Pa was a smart man. He knew I wasn't like him. I don't want the same things he did. I wouldn't mind havin' a ranch to run later on, but not one that will steal everything else out of my life like it did his. And first I want to do some traveling. After that, I'd like to go back East and go to school. I'll come back, but I want to do some livin' first. I'm not bein' generous. I'm bein' selfish, Mr. Macklin, I'm thinkin' of me. And you're the only one who can help me."

"What's your plan?"

"I don't know. You're real good at comin' up with plans—what do you think would work?"

Macklin didn't need to think about it. He said, "Tony, you're land-poor. You've got too much land and not enough cattle. Let's sell off some of the range and use the money to restock. There'll be plenty of cash left over for you to go to school. I suggest you do that first, and then you can go off and see the world if you still want to. I'll run the ranch while you're gone, and we'll be half partners. I know a good lawyer in Charleston who can draw up the papers so it will all be legal and your interests will be protected."

By the time Macklin finished speaking, Tony was grinning.

⁓⁓⁓

Cliff Doyle could tell the outlaw hideout was empty long before he and his two weary men rode into the yard. There were no horses in the corral or pasture. No smoke issued from the chimney. The place looked dead.

He had no idea how dead.

Inside the house, there was dried blood everywhere. Chairs were overturned, there were bullet holes in the walls, a window was broken. Doyle went outside and found, on a low hill behind the house, what he was sure would be there: a long row of earth mounds. He counted them and realized the entire gang was accounted for here. They had been wiped out. Had they killed each other? Had a posse come and done it?

He would never know.

Had Doyle walked up the hill and to a place on the other side—a pretty place with a long vista—he would have found another mound, and it was the only one with a marker. The name that had been scratched on the marker was that of Owen Meeker. The marker was a thin plank, and the name was shallowly carved. The elements would soon erase the carved letters and in a few years, the plank itself would rot away, and no one who came to this place would remember Owen Meeker or know he was buried here.

Doyle walked back to his horse and wearily pulled himself into the saddle. His purpose in coming here had been to persuade Ben Lukert and his gang to join him in an attack on Star Ranch, in which they would wipe out Tony Nolan and his entire crew and then divide the spoils between them.

He sat there on his horse for a long time, finally accepting the fact that he had lost everything; wondering what he would do now. He was growing older and lately had begun to feel the loss of motivating drive within him. The desire for wealth that he had always possessed was still there; in fact, recently it had become something like a frantic need, based upon the realization that his years were running out, but the driving force he had always possessed was waning. And suddenly, recognizing this, he was desperately afraid of the future; of growing old in poverty as he had seen so many men do.

He did not know in which direction to ride. He was completely out of ideas. As he sat there, flanked by the last two members of the Double H crew, the whole sequence of recent events passed through his mind, and it became clear to him that he was not quite finished here. He would have to leave the area, but there was one final thing he must do before he did.

Macklin and Sterling were having supper with Johnny Belmont in Hopkins' Restaurant in Contention. They had just finished telling him all about what Sterling proudly referred to as, "Me and Dave's adventures."

Belmont said, "Well I guess this puts an end to your crazy plan to go to Oregon."

"Never really wanted to go there anyway," said Macklin. "An Arizona man wouldn't know how to act in all that rain."

"Who knows?" said Belmont. "Maybe those Oregon gals ain't as choosy as gals down here are, and you could find yourself a wife."

Trying to get into the joke, Sterling said, "Maybe a blind gal." He laughed hard.

Macklin said, "Boys, I could find ten pretty gals who'd marry me before either of you two flop ears could find one."

Stepping out of the restaurant into the night air, Macklin felt a tingle in his belly. Something was wrong. Sterling was walking on one side of him, and Belmont was on the other side of Sterling. Macklin was about to speak when the night erupted in gunfire.

Sterling dropped like a stone. Macklin's gun was out, and he was firing at the muzzle flashes he could see. To his left, he was aware of Belmont's gun roaring.

Belmont shouted, "Get back inside," and then he flinched, spun around, and fell against the wall of the saloon.

Macklin seized Belmont's arm and dragged him into the darkness between the restaurant and an adjacent building. "You all right, Johnny?" The reply he got was incoherent, the voice gradually fading out.

Now Macklin heard the sound of running horses. Men were shouting. He ran around to the front of the restaurant and yelled, "Somebody get the doc."

His gun was still in his hand, he was still wary, but no further shots were fired. There was a group of men standing over Sterling, and Macklin ran to them. One of them said, "Dave, he's dead."

Dr. Pope had heard the shots. He came running across the street now, and Macklin ran back to where Belmont lay and checked him. He was alive.

"Stand back, Dave," said the doctor.

After a few moments, Pope said, "Some of you men pick him up and carry him to my place."

"Do you need a door, Doc?" asked one of them.

"No. Just carry him."

Macklin's and Sterling's horses were at the livery stable—unsaddled for the night. He ran around front and untied the reins of two horses that were tied there. Just then, Herman Chilter walked up, and as Macklin stepped into a saddle, he said, "Herman, I need a couple of favors."

"What is it, Dave?"

Macklin lifted up his shirt and removed his money belt. Tossing it to the butcher, he said, "Find whoever owns these horses and pay for them. Tell Don Struggs I'll take care of the kid's funeral expenses. I want Mrs. Pennington and her niece to make the arrangements. I want it to be a good one."

And he reined the horses around and thundered down the street and out into the desert.

Not just any man could stay on the trail of his quarry at night using only his senses of smell and hearing, but Macklin was not just any man. He followed in this manner, stopping frequently for brief periods, smelling the dust of those he followed and listening to the hoofbeats of their horses. And when daylight came, he was still on their trail.

Every couple of hours, he switched horses on the run, not even bothering to stop, merely leaping from one saddle to the other. The men he was following—and he had no doubt it was Cliff Doyle and his remaining Double H men—surely must know they were being followed and would do everything they could to stay ahead—at least until they realized they were only being followed by one man, as opposed to a full posse.

He fervently wished there had been time to gather some provisions and get his carbine and ammunition before following Sterling's killers, but he had known that if they got too far ahead of him, he would have to wait until daylight to track them.

Shortly after sunrise, from the top of a rise in the trail, Macklin got his first, distant look at the men he was pursuing. There were three of them, with two pack animals. The pack horses were loaded lightly; the Texans had clearly planned to travel fast. They had found a water hole, and at this moment were watering their animals. At this time of year, especially in wet years like this one had been, there were springs and water holes all over the desert, most of which would dry up after the rains stopped or at the latest by May or June of next year.

Now that he had found the Double H men, Macklin did not know how to proceed. To charge directly at them would be suicide. He pulled back, hoping they hadn't seen him, and decided to keep up with them during the day and wait for darkness to come before making a move. He was tired and hungry. He wondered how Johnny Belmont was doing, wondered if he was still alive. He thought of Sterling, and a hot anger rose up within him. He had been fond of that kid.

All morning he followed the tracks of the Texans, watching their dust in the clear air, using it to gauge their distance from him. They had not yet stopped to rest or cook a meal, but sooner or later they would have to.

It was midday when he quit seeing dust and knew they had stopped. There was a spring nearby that he knew of. They were probably fixing themselves a meal and giving their horses a rest. There was the possibility, however, that they had seen him and were waiting to ambush him. He would have to be careful.

Dave Macklin was not new to this game. He had hunted men and been hunted by them before this. He was always careful to watch his back trail, and now he saw a light wisp of dust behind him, and farther back, more dust. He moved behind cover, dismounted, waited and watched. They would come at him from two or more directions, he knew. He had two of the Texans spotted, but where was the third? From which direction would he come?

Scanning the area, he searched for the spot that would be the most advantageous for him, found it, and went there, tying his horses to a nearby paloverde tree. He wished fervently that he had a rifle. Now he waited, watching for any little amount of dust that would betray the location of that third Texan.

He tried to figure out their strategy. The dust farther back down the trail was the thing he didn't understand. It worried him. Ever alert, constantly watching, he waited.

It came from behind him—he heard a slight scuffing sound, like a boot on dirt. He moved deeper into the brush and waited. When next he heard the man, he was closer. Macklin adjusted his own position, and shortly the man emerged from the brush, cresting the hill, his rifle in his hand. He saw Macklin and swung the rifle, and Macklin shot him. The man went backward, rolling head over heels down the side of the steep hill until he was out of sight in the brush below. Macklin wanted the man's rifle, but it had gone down the hill with its owner.

Now Macklin had only two enemies to worry about, and he knew their positions. The problem was, they also knew his. He moved again, attempting to place himself in a better position. Again, he watched and waited. When he was sure it was safe, he would go down and try to recover the rifle of the man he had just shot. For now, he waited.

The distant rider was closer now—Macklin could see the man, not just his dust. The closer one had gone under cover, but Macklin knew where he was. There was something about the farther man that bothered him. Something wasn't right.

And then he knew. He recognized the horse, knew the reason for the white bandage around the rider's head precluding the wearing of a hat.

It was Johnny Belmont.

The realization of who the rider was brought another instantaneous realization—an alarming one: There was one Texan who was not accounted for. It was at that moment that Macklin felt the sting of the bullet as it burned his neck and heard the report of the rifle. Dropping to the ground, he rolled over the rim of the hill.

Where had the shot come from? He tried to remember from which direction the sound of the report had come but could only make a rough approximation.

There were rifle shots down below. Either Johnny was in trouble, or the Texan was. Right now all Macklin could do was hope Johnny could stay alive while he, Macklin, took care of his own problem.

A sound came from below. A cry of, "I'm hit Cliff. I'm hit. Need your help."

Now, Macklin knew who had shot at him. What would Cliff Doyle do now? he asked himself. He must know that Macklin had killed one of his men, and now Belmont had shot the other one. He surely knew he was the only one left. Would he attack, or would he flee?

Macklin took a chance. He raised up and started off on the run, heading for the spring, where he was certain the Texans had left their horses. He was halfway down the slope when he caught sight of Doyle, ahead of him, running in the same direction. He was going to try to get away.

The distance was too great for pistol accuracy, but Macklin sent several bullets at the Texan, and Doyle sent several at him, none of which scored a hit.

When he rounded the hill above the spring, Macklin saw that Doyle was just finished saddling a horse. Doyle saw him and sent a few wild shots at him, his pistol hammer finally clicking on an empty chamber. Then, in frantic haste, he sprang into the saddle.

Macklin was still too far away for an accurate pistol shot, but he stopped, steadied himself, and fired the last two bullets in his gun. Doyle's horse stopped and staggered. The Texan spurred it savagely, but the horse could not move.

It was then that Macklin saw that the Texan, in his hurry, had left his rifle leaning against a rock. Doyle leaped clear of the saddle and sprinted toward the weapon.

Now Macklin had a split-instant decision to make. He could take time to reload his pistol or run for Doyle's rifle, hoping he could get there before Doyle did. He chose the latter, knowing that at this range, the man with the rifle would have the advantage. Doyle reached the rifle first, but Macklin was on him, grasping the rifle, not giving him a chance to bring it to bear.

They grappled for a few seconds, and Macklin head-butted the big man and began pushing him backward. Doyle finally released his grip on the rifle, but he swung a hard fist at Macklin's head, connecting with the side of the face, and Macklin's vision clouded. This Texan was a powerful man.

Macklin drove forward as his vision cleared, dropping the rifle, wrapping his arms around Doyle's waist, trying to keep him from the weapon, holding blindly to the man, nearly lifting him off the ground as Macklin's legs drove against the ground like pistons.

Something tripped Doyle, and he fell backward. Macklin took advantage of this, sitting atop Doyle, throwing vicious punches into his face. Doyle was not beaten, however, and he swung his big fists with fearsome effect, finally knocking Macklin off him. Exhausted, the two men struggled to their knees, and Doyle swung again. Macklin blocked the punch, not wanting to receive another of those sledge-hammer blows.

They were next to the spring now, and Macklin pulled his feet under him and lunged at Doyle, knocking him on his back, his head and shoulders landing in the water. Macklin used the weight of his body to push the big Texan's head under and hold it there. Doyle struggled fiercely for his life, bucking and arching his back, trying to throw Macklin off. He kicked and scraped the dirt with his spurs, he hammered at Macklin's head with his big fists until Macklin was nearly unconscious.

Macklin's only advantage now was the position of his body atop Doyle's. The blows Doyle rained on his head and body gradually decreased in frequency and force until, finally, they stopped altogether.

Macklin tried to pull himself away, but he simply lacked the strength. He lay there, gulping air, until he drifted into sleep or unconsciousness. He never knew which.

Through the fog in his mind, Macklin heard the sounds of a wood fire crackling. Soon he began to smell coffee. He opened his eyes and waited for his vision to clear, afterward forcing himself, with trembling muscles, to sit up, aware that omeone had rolled him clear of the body of Cliff Doyle. He looked around. Johnny Belmont was there, making coffee. He looked at Macklin and said, "You pick interestin' times and places to take a siesta."

Not trusting his legs, Macklin crawled over to the fire. "I need some of that coffee."

They sat and drank the coffee for a while, neither of them speaking. Presently Macklin, more mentally alert now, noticed the bloody, makeshift bandage on Belmont's leg.

He said, "Johnny, you are just a magnet for lead."

Belmont shook his head at the irony. "Seems like if there's any of it flyin' around, I catch it."

"Speakin' of which, how's the head?"

Belmont chuckled. "Doc Pope said it was lucky the bullet didn't hit me in some vital area."

"I'm surprised he let you go."

"He didn't. But he couldn't stop me neither."

There was silence as they drank the coffee, and finally, Belmont said, "Sorry about Sterling."

Macklin said, "He was just a dumb kid. He . . ." Macklin shook his head.

They sat in silence again for a time. Later they would eat some of Doyle's food, but for now, neither of them felt like preparing a meal.

Presently Belmont said, "You'll have to play at bein' marshal of Contention again until I get walkin' on both legs."

"Not this time, Johnny."

"It'll just be for a couple of weeks, Dave."

"Nope. I'm a rancher now. I've got responsibilities."

"Tony and his crew can handle it until you get out there."

"No, Johnny. I won't do it."

There was another pause, and Macklin said, "Think you can make it back to town?"

"Think you can? Your face looks like a fresh hide—which don't change your looks much at all."

"In your case, it would be an improvement."

Later, as Macklin was helping him onto his horse, Belmont said from out of nowhere, "Have you ever noticed how pretty Lena Carlson is?"

"Yep."

"I'm takin' her to the dance next Saturday night."

Macklin looked pointedly at Belmont's bandaged leg. "I'll dance with her for you."

"I'll do my own dancin', bad leg or not."

"You treat that girl right, Johnny, or I'll shoot you in the other leg."

CHAPTER 9

Dave Macklin had taken a couple of hours off from his duties as acting marshal of Contention City and was playing a game of checkers with Johnny Belmont at Dr. Pope's place, when Paul Bitner walked into the room.

"I was told you would be here, Dave," said Bitner.

After the usual greetings, Bitner said, "I'm leaving Arizona. I got promoted to major, and I'm being transferred to Fort Robinson in Nebraska."

Macklin and Belmont both offered their congratulations.

Bitner thanked them and said, "I need a favor, Dave. I came to say goodbye to some people. I wasn't given permission to come here, and I've missed the stage to Tucson. I can catch up to it at Three Cottonwoods, but I'll have to leave my horse there. I was wondering if you could go get it and make sure the army gets it back."

"No."

"You won't do that for me?"

"I'll go get the horse, but I'll give it back just like the army gave me back my horses."

Bitner laughed. "You'd better do a good job of changing the brand. That U.S. brand stands out."

Macklin followed Bitner outside. There was something he wanted to know but didn't know how to ask. He said, "Any plans of coming back here?"

"Not if I can help it."

"Have you said goodbye to Mrs. Pennington?"

Bitner looked directly at him. "What is it you want to know, Dave?"

"Nothing that's any of my business."

Paul Bitner felt the bile of jealousy rise up within him. He had just said goodbye to Nan White, knowing he'd never see her again, convinced that she loved Dave Macklin, and, though he knew he was being petty, he wasn't feeling particularly benevolent toward Macklin at the moment. He said, "Maybe you aren't as unlucky in love as you think, Dave. Maybe you're just a plain old ordinary fool." He swung into the saddle and rode away, leaving Macklin standing there.

The recent events involving Dave Macklin had become popular topics of discussion in Contention, and whenever they were brought up in the presence of Elona Chilter, she made disparaging comments about Macklin, hating the fact that he was so well-regarded.

Ever since Macklin had returned to Contention City, Johnny Belmont had teased him mercilessly about the fact that he had told everyone in town he was going to Oregon, had sold or given away nearly everything he owned, and then had gotten no farther away than Benson. Now, as Macklin boarded the stage for Three Cottonwoods to retrieve Paul Bitner's horse, Belmont said to him, "Off to Oregon again?"

"Yep," said Macklin, good-naturedly, "Wish me luck."

Standing in the doorway of the butchershop, Elona Chilter witnessed the exchange. Later, as Nan and Sally were strolling along Main Street, they were hailed by Elona. They stepped into the shop, and she said to Sally, "I hope you didn't loan any money to Dave Macklin, because you'll never get it back."

"How's that?" asked Sally.

"He's gone. Run off."

Nan was not sure whether to believe this or not, but when she asked where Macklin had gone and was told he had gone to Oregon, the story took on a ring of truth.

"When did he leave?" she asked Elona.

"About an hour ago, on the Tucson stage."

Somehow Nan found herself outside, and by the time Sally, with her short, thick legs, caught up with her, she was almost to the stage office.

Sally said, "Are you going to do what I think you are, Nan?"

Nan rounded on her, her eyes flashing, "Aunt Sally, I'm not chasing him, I just need to talk to him. Don't try to stop me."

Sally laughed. "My dear, you don't know me very well. I'll pay for your ticket."

In recent months, two new stage lines had sprung up to compete with John D. Kinnear's original company. As a result of this trade war, there were now three stages a day between Tucson and the Tombstone area, instead of just two a week.

Nan bought a ticket on the next stage for Tucson and, after a short wait, it arrived. She boarded the coach and sat next to the window. Sally came up to the window and took her hand and said, "Do you remember when I told you I knew who you were supposed to marry?"

"Yes, Aunt Sally. And I know too. That's why I'm going."

Macklin didn't follow the stage road back to Contention City; he didn't have to. Riding Paul Bitner's U.S. Cavalry mount—he was able to cut across the desert, following the straightest line. When he arrived, he immediately went to Sally Pennington's house, resolved to finally speak with Nan about his feelings for her. When he got there, Sally came to the sitting room where he had been taken and said, "Mr. Macklin. This is a surprise. We were told you had left for Oregon."

"Who in the world told you that?"

"Elona Chilter."

Macklin shook his head in disgust. "Herman needs to beat that woman."

"No he doesn't, and if you ever beat Nan, I'll take a broomstick to you."

Macklin was confused by this statement. Was she saying what he thought she was? He said, "I'm not sure I understand."

Sally threw up her hands. "Oh, for Heaven's sake. I am so tired of you and Nan dancing around and hiding your feelings. Don't you know that girl loves you?"

"Well, I—"

"And are you finally willing to come out and say you love her?"

He hesitated for just a moment before saying, "Yes."

"Then tell her."

"That's why I came here. Can I see her?"

Sally laughed. She laughed long and hard, releasing all her own pent-up emotions. Finally, she said, "You two are going to put me in an early grave. No, she's not here. She took the stage to Tucson. She was following you. And, if . . ." she stopped.

He was already out the door, running for his horse.

The stage pulled into the Three Cottonwoods Station for a change of horses and to allow the passengers to stretch their legs. Nan climbed out of the coach and walked toward the station She had been wondering if Paul Bitner had made it in time to catch the stage, and as she passed Mel Walker, bringing out fresh horses, she said, "Mr. Walker, did Major Bitner catch the stage before it left?"

"Sure did, ma'am. And Dave Macklin came and picked up his horse."

Surprised by this unexpected piece of news, she said, "How did he pick up the horse? I thought he came on the stage."

"He did, ma'am, and he left on the major's horse."

"Did he ride to Tucson?"

"No ma'am. He went east. He wasn't going to Tucson."

So, that was the end. She had missed him. He was gone from her life. She felt like a fool. Why had she thought she could catch up with him? And even if she had succeeded, what had she expected to accomplish? He was leaving. If a man loved a woman, would he go far away where he would never see her again?

Having made arrangements to stay overnight at Three Cottonwoods and take the morning stage back to Contention City, she stood dejectedly in the afternoon sun and watched the stage to Tucson depart without her. She could have gone on to Tucson where her mother and sister were, but neither of them would understand what she was feeling like her Aunt Sally would.

Later, sitting at a table, staring abstractedly at her untouched supper, she heard the door open and someone come in. She didn't look up; her thoughts were elsewhere. Presently she became aware of someone standing in front of her table. She looked up. Dave Macklin was there, gazing at her with an odd smile on his face.

"Mind if I sit down?" he asked.

She nodded and turned away, suddenly finding it necessary to dry her eyes with her handkerchief.

He looked away, giving her time to compose herself. Presently she turned back and smiled at him.

He said, "Surprised to see me?"

"Frankly, yes. I thought you were on your way to Oregon."

"I thought you were on your way to Tucson."

"I was, but . . ." She stopped, unwilling now to tell him why she was here.

"What was it you wanted to talk to me about if you caught up with me in Tucson?"

"How did you know I was going there to find you? . . . Oh. You must have talked to Aunt Sally."

"I did. I went there to talk to you."

Her eyes widened a little. "What about?"

He furrowed his brow pensively and said, "Just now, I can't remember. Seems like it was something important, though." He scratched his head, pretending to be struggling with his memory. And then, suddenly, he brightened. "Oh, I remember now." He sobered. All jocularity left him. He said in a voice that was both soft and tender, "I was going to ask you to marry me."

She made a sound that was half laugh, half sob, and, her eyes shining with wetness, she reached over and took his hand.

And for a long time, they sat there, looking into each other's eyes without speaking.

*

Bonus

Interested in a little more? I wrote a short story that accompanies this book, and you can get it for free on my website. The link is below, and thanks for reading!

visit

http://authorcmcurtis.com/arizona-aesop

OFFICIAL WEBSITE
authorcmcurtis.com

FOLLOW C.M. ON FACEBOOK
facebook.com/authorcmcurtis